MW01635601

SEPARATED

a novel

B. L. Mehnert

Cover photos by Susanne Lutze

Editing by Tami Jeffers

ISBN: 979-857-349-6078

Printed and bound in the United States of America

Far
We've been traveling far
Without a home
But not without a star

Free
Only want to be free
We huddle close
Hang on to a dream

On the boats and on the planes
They're coming to America
Never looking back again
They're coming to America

Home, don't it seem so far away
Oh, we're traveling light today
In the eye of the storm
In the eye of the storm

Home, to a new and a shiny place
Make our bed, and we'll say our grace
Freedom's light burning warm
Freedom's light burning warm

Got a dream to take them there
They're coming to America
Got a dream they've come to share
They're coming to America
Today, today, today, today

Neil Diamond 1980

SEPARATED

[2018]

ONE

The professor's brown pants were a little baggy, a tiny bit wrinkled, and slightly too long. They fit his character even if they didn't exactly fit his body. The overstretched neck of his wool sweater complemented the rumpled trousers with the perfect display of disregard for fashion. It wasn't that Henry Novak was a slob or a snob, the caring part of him simply wasn't indicated by his wardrobe. Henry *was* caring. He cared for his college students, his mental health clients, his only daughter, and precious grandson; he even cared about his son-in-law. Mostly, Henry cared for his wife, Marie. Literally.

Decades in academia and private practice had worn his emotions and rounded the edges of his soul. He still enjoyed seeing the occasional light bulb brighten above the head of a student in any of the post-graduate psychology classes he taught. It was near happening on this Friday afternoon and the sound of the discourse made his ears smile.

"Professor Novak, Erikson's stages-of-development-theory is carefully laid out and has been accepted since the 1950s, but unlike some of the others, it spans the lifetime and is considerably comprehensive. None of the developmental theories explain all the aspects of nature and nurture. My question is, do you think that Erikson's German background influenced him in any way toward an ideal, inclusive approach?"

"Interesting question, Emily. Why are you posing that during our Piaget lecture?" Henry reveled in the workings of his students' minds. He preferred a stimulating debate that encouraged individual reasoning over the sound of his own voice.

"About the time Erikson was a young man, Germany was fighting in World War I and just after he moved to the U.S., Germany got involved in World War II. There must have been a rumble of Aryanism in the country at that time. Do you think that influenced his theory in the longevity form that it emerged? It's different from Piaget's approach." Emily may have been trying to sidetrack the current boring discussion, but there was merit in her inquiry.

"And remind me what Piaget's approach was." Henry tested her.

"He observed his own children?" Emily's voice wavered as if she was uncertain.

"Are you asking me?" The prodding came before launching into a sidebar. "Who knows what started World War I?" A few hands sluggishly rose. "Adam."

"Some guy was assassinated, then the assassin guy was arrested. Another country wanted him, but the first country wouldn't let him go. Somehow, Germany got involved from there."

"An amazing slaughter of details. Thank you, Adam. You are not wrong." The professor smiled and sauntered toward the desk that held his textbook and chalk.

"Germany entered World War I to support Hungary. There are many reasons floating around about World War II. Have you heard of Adolf Hitler?" The question garnered a subdued snicker across the lecture hall. "Hitler fought in the first world war as a young man. Some believe him to be obsessed with the deaths of his fellow soldiers, causing him to welcome the possibility of revenge in renewed fighting of upcoming battles. Others say he was a maniacal tyrant driven to conquer and rule more countries. Either way, we know how that story ends once he got into a position of power. The point about the tone in the country is a good topic, Emily, and I will open the discussion to the floor. What do the rest of you think about personal influences of these men like Freud, Bandura, and Piaget, who helped shape the study of behavioral development?" His arm swept over the lecture theater as an invitation.

"Aren't we all shaped by our experiences?" one brave soul questioned.

"Many of these men lived in more than one country. They probably steadily rose above their early life experiences after studying and conducting experiments," rebuffed another.

"Yeah, living in different cultures probably helped them to expand their understanding of development," offered a female student.

"Well, what about you?" Henry centered himself at the front of the ascending rows. "When you're pouring over your Human Development chapters, do any of your own experiences seep through your contemplations to reinforce or dispel the text?" He waited for answers.

"All the time," came from the left side of the room.

"Can't help it," offered someone in the third row.

"Our own experiences come to mind, but we have to rationalize if they are helpful or distracting. We need to take what we know, then apply the research," interjected a female in the back.

"So, Emily, can you answer your own question with the input from your fellow students?"

"Seems we are all influenced by our own experiences, but we decide if it affects our work or not."

"On a good day," Henry muttered.

The clock on the wall confirmed that he had once again gone over the allotted time. With his back to the students, he slapped his textbook shut. He waved his left hand above his head without looking up. No one waited for a comment as the students swarmed out of the room in a beehive of noisy escape. Henry opened the worn leather case that was so old it was called a book bag not a backpack. Sliding the text and papers inside, he brushed his fingers together, releasing a slight plume of chalk dust. He was partial to this room without the benefit of a dry erase board.

He lowered his head as he exited the classroom and absently made his way to the office he shared with another professor in the department. A clutter of papers, books, and handouts greeted him. His desk stood covered with the daily necessities of academia, leaving barely enough room to write a note. He lingered long enough to sign a document for the dean and check the schedule. His plan to leave was thwarted by a student with a grade complaint.

Henry backtracked into the office and offered her a seat. He unlocked his desk and slid out the grade book to lay atop the disorder. A quick perusal of questions and her choice of answers showed the correct were correct and the wrong were marked wrong.

A memory of this student in his Monday/Wednesday morning advanced Statistics class surfaced. She hadn't missed a session, but she hadn't been one to speak up during a lecture. Her assignments arrived on time, but each test was passed by the slightest of margins.

"What are you questioning?"

The girl cleared her throat. "Number twelve." She pointed to her sheet. "It's marked wrong, but I don't know why."

"Why don't you explain to me what you're thinking."

She chose her words carefully. “The Bernoulli trial is an example of a binomial distribution. I picked the example of flipping a coin which is a discrete distribution.”

The black on white version was sometimes difficult to gel with a student’s brain matter. Henry allowed her to express her knowledge of the subject which would indicate comprehension much better than a test question.

“Given what you know about success/failure outcomes, would you say that permutations are involved in binomial distribution?”

“No, sir. Independent trials result in one of two mutually exclusive outcomes.”

“So, using your example of flipping a coin, if I wanted to know how many times, I could flip heads out of five tosses, could the binomial distribution provide that statistic?”

“Yes, sir, that’s a common type use for it since it’s not continuous.”

Satisfied that the student understood the concept he told her, “Well, Melanie, let me hold on to this. I need to look over my test to be certain the multiple choices are valid.”

“Thank you, Professor Novak.” She spun around and out the door before he could change his mind.

Henry took the paper and slid it in the drawer with his grade book. His knuckle rubbed the bookmark his father made for him when he was a schoolboy. The thin piece of wood, sanded and generously lacquered, had taken on an amber hew with decades of rest between pages. It seemed thicker now, as if it had absorbed serious ideas and truths. The touch of it managed a warm recollection. He locked the compartment and headed to the parking lot.

He reached his tan Ford Focus caked with the slush from iced and snowy roads, opened the trunk, and tossed his book bag next to the jack and the jumper cables. Friday was his shortest day of the work week. It meant he could get home to his wife and start the weekend.

The slow pace of the car matched his energy capacity as he rolled through the narrow streets of the campus and merged onto the highway of throbbing traffic, steaming pavement, and blaring horns. Daydreams snuck up on him. His fingers frantically tapped on the steering wheel, and his brain skimmed images of credit card bills. Expenses and doctor visits marched across his mind's eye. Familiar dreads sang to him like a chorus while he drove. *Are there enough hours to work in one week to meet my obligations? Can I squeeze in a few more counseling sessions?* The answers were all there, but he needed them to change. Things were just not working as they were. *How long would it take before the bottom fell out?*

TWO

"Miss Nadia, I'm home." Henry closed the wooden door to the apartment.

A lively woman, short in stature, zipped around the corner, buttoning her coat with purse in hand. Nadia Koscka didn't trouble him with chit chat. Her day was not ending, even if Henry's was winding down.

"Everything went well today, Mr. Novak. Miss Marie had a fine day. The mail is on the table in the kitchen. Dinner is on the stove. The trash is here, and I'll toss it on my way out. You have a nice weekend now. Bye." Her old Polish accent was as cheerful as her round face while she hustled through the door.

"Thank you, Miss Nadia. I'll see you on Monday," he called after her. Whistling a melody, he learned from his father, Henry placed the old book bag in his converted office.

The shelves of yellowing manuals and papers reached nearly to the ceiling. Designed to be a bedroom, it had adapted to the rearrangement in the apartment three years prior. Precious framed pictures of the family reflecting smiling faces during happy times were propped up amid the psychology texts and reference material. Some photos were recent while the ones from the old country, although scratched and faded, retained their exclusive corner. A red ball with worn creases where the rubber gave way to cracks waited on the shelf next to a beaming photo of its six-year-old owner. His grampa picked it up from its place, revealing dust and neglect on the shelf beneath. Bouncing it once on the floor, he squeezed it as hard as his tired fingers could and continued squeezing as he stepped down the short hall and into the living room.

"Matka, I'm home. How are you doing?" He leaned over the figure lying in the bed and kissed her gently on the forehead. "Miss Nadia said you had a fine day." He continued talking as he side-stepped around the bed. "What did you girls talk about? C'mon tell me, I won't breathe a word." Fussing with the blanket that covered her thin frame, he stroked her stiff, delicate hand before bringing it to his lips.

"You said what?" he asked in shock. "Then what did she say? On no, you're kidding." Placing the red ball next to her hand, he glanced over the remarks on a clip board that lay on a side table that used to hold the dinner china.

"Looks like you had a great dinner. Did you save anything for me? Got a bath too. Right here in the living room? How scandalous. The neighbors will talk. . ." With that he rested the clip board next to the medicinal cream and medicated powder that had replaced the cholinesterase inhibitors as the final stage prescriptions. He lit an aromatherapy candle and switched on the phonograph to hear a gentle classic melody then walked the few paces that led to the open kitchen.

The simmering beef and vegetables floated a tasty tease across the air. He reached for a bowl and a spoon and ladled a generous helping. He poured a glass of milk, salted his food, and eased his rumpled body in front of the meal. Before the first bite, his eyes closed, and head bowed in thanks for the dinner, his family, and his job. He tasted Miss Nadia's hearty stew.

The mail remained untouched on the table. There was no need to open the envelopes to know their contents. Eventually, Henry rose from his seat and moved to the sink. He washed his dishes, wiped the table, and tidied the counter, then moved back to the gray living room where his wife lay quietly.

"Do you need anything, Matka?" he asked softly. With gentle hands he lifted the coverlet and reached under until he felt the plastic around her waist. Satisfied that she was comfortable and dry he told her, "Let me get my papers, and I'll be right back."

His footsteps were heavier now as he found his way back to the office that housed volumes of reference material, research papers, tomes of psychological theories, and manuscripts hoping for publication. His first glance always rested upon the family pictures and the smiles that peeked back. He removed a mass of papers from his weathered book bag and picked up a red pen and a ballpoint before returning to the former living room.

He perched on the edge of the vinyl recliner before sliding back into a comfortable position. All that he needed was within reach. Papers were spread on his lap, the remote was within his grasp and, most importantly, he could touch his wife. One by one he read each submission, considering the words carefully, weeding out the bullshit from facts. The class discussion was most enjoyable and gauged the participation of the individuals sitting in the rows. Some surprised him with silence in the lecture hall but displayed astonishing insight into the subject by offering in depth oral presentations. The young minds were a constant source of energy for his waning enthusiasm.

Two hours of grading and correcting passed while Henry squirmed to occasionally regain a comfortable position in his chair. Each time he did so, he bent to ask his wife if she was also comfortable.

"Still doing alright, Matka?" he would ask while patting her hand.

She had not answered him in nearly three years. It had been a slow degeneration which gave the family ample time to adjust but it didn't make it easy. Henry dismissed the early forgetfulness and lapses when the memories faded along with simple daily routines. He would find a container of ice cream melting in the cupboard or a pencil in the refrigerator. She called him by her brother's name. The last several years took their toll when she no longer remembered her own name, could not get herself dressed, then lost her speech.

Marie's angelic voice had drawn Henry to her in the beginning. He was working on his Ph.D. with little time for anything but classes. A friend dragged him to a campus concert to get him out of their apartment. It was there that Henry fell off the cliff into love at first sight.

A diminutive five foot two, brown-haired, vision of a girl walked on stage and sat at the grand piano. Her fingers glided along the keys and created lilting melodies that filled the music hall. But when she sang, the audience, especially Henry, fell silent in adoration. It transformed him. It had been months since he had concentrated on anything other than psychology and behavior and mental capacity or physical response. He experienced a physical response of his own at the sight of the beautiful and talented girl on the stage.

He was twenty-five, and she was twenty-three. The pursuit was on. He was hopelessly enchanted and reduced to a helpless sap during a clumsy courtship. He completed his studies and she hers. They married, had a beautiful daughter a few years later, and lived happily ever after. Henry continued to believe the happily ever after, even now as he grieved the loss of his lovely and gifted wife.

"I need to stand and stretch my legs. How about you? Do you need to stretch, Matka?" It took some effort for Henry to push himself out of the chair that would tend to swallow him. He left the graded papers to stand straight and adjust his baggy trousers. His fingers ran along her covers as he walked out of the room.

In a moment, he returned with a bottle, a glass, and a spoon. He carefully poured about two inches of liquid into the glass and set it on the side table. He addressed his wife. With a few drops on the spoon, he leaned over her rigid form. He lifted her gray head in one hand and tenderly slid the spoon between her lips. The drops fell inside her mouth. When they had been safely absorbed, he replaced her head then raised his glass.

"A toast to us!" Down went the Schnapps.

He tidied the kitchen again, washed his hands, and returned to his wife.

"Let me get you comfortable." He pulled the covers back from her body and spoke softly while he changed her disposable underwear. He washed her thin and delicate flesh with veins like roads on a map and repositioned her bony form. She was barely ninety pounds. The mental toll amounted to a heavier burden.

"Is that better? Let's get you covered up and snuggled in." With that he tucked the blanket around her, propped a pillow against her back, and slipped each arm underneath the covers. "You are all set now. Sleep tight." He noticed the newest bed sore beginning to form near her hip.

With one last kiss for the night, Henry sighed and walked toward the bedroom, which was barely three steps farther than the recliner. Each room of the small apartment allowed for quick access to where his wife lay. He was in the middle of undressing when a groan from the living room startled him.

"Aaaaaa." Silence. "Ohhhh." Henry rushed to the bedside. Nothing had changed. Marie had not moved. Yet the sound of her occasional guttural groans always startled him.

"Aaaaaa." The throaty sound came from deep within.

Henry touched her softly. The sound meant nothing, but it chilled him. "Matka, tell me," he asked her. "How can I help? It sounds so painful."

Silence. Stillness and silence.

Henry stood next to his wife's hospital bed, dressed only in his pajama bottoms. His bare feet stood on the cold floor. Walls were getting closer, debt rising higher, darkness sealing them up. His mind was a swirl of worries. When she made sounds, these unnatural sounds, so unlike her sweet voice, the essence of her true self was buried farther away than ever.

"What can I do?" He pleaded for an answer. His pulse eased toward normal when he understood nothing had harmed her and bending close to her ear he whispered, "Matka, I'm so tired." He went to the bedroom and pulled on his pajama top.

THREE

The room was one of roughly six hundred in the neo-classical building connected by miles of corridors. Inside were lofty ceilings, curved rows of leather chairs behind polished, dark, wooden tables that fanned in an arc. Not every seat was presently taken.

A central chair at the front table was assigned for the current witness. Amenities included a pitcher of iced water, an array of glasses, writing essentials, and a stationary microphone. In front of those rows were laden humans sprawled out with hefty distracting cameras and annoying microphone booms stationed to catch each word, hiccup, and hard swallow. Behind the middle ground of photographers and journalists, was a single arc of tables with men and women waiting to ask and be answered. The gentleman in the center of that main position was the chairman at this round of congressional hearings.

Of the eight hundred and fifty doorways in the Capitol building, a handful opened and closed continuously in this room, beginning at 8:00 a.m. EDT allowing spectators, senators, congressmen and women, staffers, and expected witnesses to enter and exit. The constant interruption of noise and distraction detracted from the importance of the topic. It was a typical day on the Hill.

Rising with measured pace, the congressman scanned the seats to his right and left, more with a shift of his eyes than a turn of his head. He tried to flex and stretch without being conspicuous. He had listened intently for more than two hours as questions were asked, and witnesses read from written testimony while interspersing mildly derogatory or complimentary comments in their remarks. It all depended on the political affiliation of who subpoenaed them. Stuart Samson could pretty much predict what direction the speakers would lean before they said a word. He dropped into the hearing, as he always tried to do when it concerned immigration, to get a feel of what was currently transpiring.

This hearing would drag on for most of the rest of this day at least; no doubt, several more days. His chief of staff had blocked out these last hours for the congressman to indulge himself. Now it was time to get back to his office. His calendar mentally displayed like Tony Stark's computer screen, and his attention had shifted to the afternoon meetings on his own schedule.

A stern countenance and broad shoulders provided a menacing profile of which Stuart was often unaware. Four years as a cadet at the Naval Academy, followed by sixteen years as a software engineer for the Navy, had disciplined him. Even now, he ascribed to daily workouts and a vigilant diet.

When he ended his military career, he enthusiastically embraced politics, conducting his government duties with insight and determination, and meeting challenges head on. His duties as a young congressman found Stuart working long hours, but his eagerness to educate others in government, his constituency, and elsewhere about the benefits of diversification never ceased.

He was in the middle of his third term as House representative from Ohio and re-election motivated only about twenty-five percent of his actions. He was apt to think he was a servant of the people, feeling pride and pressure in equal turns.

When he was a new representative in the House, he had asked, solicited, appealed, requested, and bargained to be recommended to serve on the standing committee that would allow him to influence, even at the slightest amount, immigration oversight. The appointment had only recently been offered to him.

“How did it go sir?” Peter Basefield waited inside the office when Stuart arrived.

“Well, Peter, what can I say? It went as expected. Over the two hours I got a brief glimpse of the latest testimony regarding the immigration situation. Lots more to come.”

Stuart dropped into his swivel chair and moved it from side to side in irritation. He stopped to pick up a pen from his desk, adjusted his glasses, and glanced through the spotless window in his small office. He spoke in a murmur more to himself than to the young man waiting before him. “Thousands of children are being separated from their parents since the “zero tolerance” immigration policy was implemented.” He mumbled the ideas tumbling in his head at the same time he rummaged through papers in his in-box.

"Descriptions of the process and procedures . . . discouraging. Pictures coming out of the Associated Press . . . awful conditions . . . further administration plans to erect a "tent city. They're talking about converting another abandoned warehouse . . ."

Stuart focused on his computer screen and his further reflections commenced inside his head. Peter returned to his own desk outside the room. The latest factors acted as catalysts for Stuart's resolve to be part of development and execution of a more humane process.

Even as Stuart instigated plans to act on his ideas for improvement, he grounded himself to the matters at hand. He first gave his attention to his lunch calendar hoping that the afternoon meeting with his home state committee on education would provide a more upbeat dialogue. Before he could censor himself, a resigned sigh escaped at the realization lunch included a group of blowhard lobbyists. *The life of the elected official.* He exited the planner screen.

He checked the watch on his left wrist and reached for his raincoat. An automatic reflex found him examining his back pocket to be sure his wallet hadn't jumped out and slid between the cushions of his chair. On the other side of the office door, he stopped in front of Peter Basefield's desk.

"I'm having lunch with a group of NPO lobbyists at Charlie Palmer's." He used the initials for

Non-Profit Organization. "Do you have the number there in case you need me?" He wrestled with his coat sleeve. The polite habit to turn off his cell phone completely when in a meeting came from respect and hating to be interrupted.

"Yes, sir. I booked your reservation."

"I won't be back to the office today. There is a meeting at 2:00 with Ohio reps that will branch into sub-groups and possibly take the rest of the day. Get in touch with me if anything comes up. Thanks. Oh, and don't forget to get a copy of the minutes from today's budget meeting for me. I'll need it first thing tomorrow morning. Going to be an early day." He was gone.

Peter shuffled a stack of papers to the right of his computer, entered a prompt, and picked up the phone. His own days were always early.

FOUR

"Let's take a look at the area that's troubling you." Dr. Priscilla Harris-Hunt moved closer to Jamison Corlander, seated with his back to her in front of an open textbook on the small table. She leaned over his broad shoulder and lightly rubbed her breast against him. A whiff of her expensive perfume engulfed him as he looked up. Her attentive face posed so close to his.

"The two theories are contradictory," he offered his well laid out contention. "I can see both points and can't reconcile them." He struggled to concentrate with her so near, her breath bouncing off his neck. Did she know she was making it difficult for his lungs to work?

"Maybe we need to take a closer look," she suggested and reached across his chest to turn some pages. Her perfectly manicured nails touched the paper with the delicacy of a ballerina's port de bras.

"Show me where you think the discrepancy lies." Her voice dripped with interest and the warmth of her words touched the skin on his jaw. Jamison squirmed awkwardly in the chair as she leaned above.

"Here, let me stand and you can sit. Be more comfortable." Raising his athletic frame became an ungainly proposition in the tight space where Dr. Harris-Hunt had suggested they review his questions. There were psychology lecture halls, classrooms, and lab rooms, and then there was this closet-like space behind the last classroom that Jamison didn't even know existed. She instructed him to meet her here, claiming it would be less noisy. With his six-foot-two frame and near two-hundred-pound body, the visual of a bull in a china shop charged through his mind.

Finally, unfolding to his full length, he offered his professor the use of the chair, but the pretty woman stood still, looking up at him. The silence was disconcerting, but she had been correct; it was quiet in there. He remained the object of her view. A waft of her rich perfume once again teased his senses, and an unbelievable notion crossed his mind. *Could she be...?*

Before he could finish the inconceivable sentence in his brain, the door to the room flew open and a giggling co-ed loaded with books walked in, looked at the two of them, giggled again, and swung around. The door slammed shut. Embarrassment engulfed Jamison as he expected the girl, whoever she was, might be thinking who knows what about seeing them there. He centered his attention back to Professor Harris-Hunt and she now stood closer than before.

"Well, I guess this room isn't as private as it once was." She didn't sound bothered. "Why don't you let me take your paper with me? I'll look it over thoroughly and we can discuss it tomorrow. How does that sound?" She leisurely gathered up her things.

"Sure, great." Jamison stammered. "I have practice after my classes. Um, I can..."

"Come by my office at 7:00 p.m. You'll be done with practice by then I expect." She had already slid by him, rubbing her pink bouclé suit against his ass in the process. He listened for the sound of her heels down the hall, needing a little time while he collected himself, and his things. Finally, he let out his breath.

* * *

Priscilla made her way to the department reception space to pick up mail and copies of the test scheduled on the syllabus for the following week. Farther down the tiled corridor, she stopped in front of the office she shared with Dr. Henry Novak. She manipulated the key into the lock and glided through the door, setting the tests on the left side of her organized desk.

Her section of the room boasted several awards for research, along with framed prestigious journal clippings, and MENSA membership credentials, that she displayed prominently on a shelf alongside various other academic acknowledgements. A few mounted photos adorned her wall. There hung the one of the university president and her. One of the Dean of the Department of Education with her. She reached to center the one of the governor of the state of Virginia beside her.

Her officemate, Dr. Novak, had a more laissez faire attitude. Thorough as he may have been in his duties, she often wondered how he could navigate with such terrible feng shui. Although their approach to life and work differed, she remained grateful for his routine which included punctuality and predictability as a hallmark. When the day ended, he usually left the office allowing her semi-privacy. In that single respect, their pair up proved advantageous.

She sorted her mail, and the first envelope held a request for a letter of recommendation. An easy memory of the student surfaced, a handsome young man, ambitious and motivated, with good grades, impressive test scores, and killer eyelashes. A positive letter would be easy to compose because of a template on her computer that she used for such letters, simply filling in personal details for the individual students. It made life easier.

The second envelope housed a brief note of gratitude from a former student, now doing well in her entry level job at a community mental health facility. The face of this student didn't come to mind as quickly, not that she was losing a step. *Fifty is the new thirty. I get a pass for not remembering every student.* She moved on to the next envelope.

Knowing that each professor had to accumulate continuing education units to keep their skills and licensure up to date by law, the Dean of the Department of Education had procured spots for several of the staff to attend a four-day seminar. Arranged by the dean and endorsed by the Chairman of the Psychology Department, Dr. Douglas Yantz,

Priscilla received word that the upcoming seminar would be taking place in a few short weeks.

A proposal of leaving the classroom for a few days didn't worry her nor could she honestly state that abandoning her husband would give her pause. What did keep finding its way to the top of her concern was the effort she had put into the priming of Jamison Corlander and that her charms of persuasion were just about to pay off.

Priscilla calculated that she had seduced him to the point of melting the awkward exterior of his youth and naiveté. His arousal was evident when their bodies lingered close and the cheeky visual caused her to uncross and re-cross her legs. Experience informed her that she could initiate that final move and what delightful adventures would follow.

Boredom with her wealth and entitlement had set in years before. There was a brief affair with a charming business associate of her husband's company. Admittedly, it was not so much the man himself or the companionship but the thrill of the game that enticed her. When the tryst abruptly ended, she had not been dismayed. Rather, she trolled for the next prize, looking close to work at the prospects half her age. Jamison was the epitome of vitality; young, strong, athletic. Being intelligent came as a bonus. The fact that he was a different race excited her more. She closed her planner without blocking off the seminar dates. Even the dean could not distract her. She would figure out an effective way to decline.

A smaller envelope had slipped from the others and now lay upon her desk. It boasted the easily identifiable university insignia. She tore through the paper and an uncharacteristic wave of sympathy swept through her when she read:

Professor,
This note is to inform you that Marie Jusua Pieski Novak, wife of our colleague, Dr. Henry Novak, has died. Services will be held on Friday, March 19, 2018 at Christ Central Church, 151 McIntire Park Drive, Charlottesville should you wish to attend. A teacher assistant will be circulating an envelope for donations and a card for you to sign. Thank you for your participation.
Dr. Douglas Yantz, Department of Psychology, Chairman

"Poor Henry. Well at least that terrible chapter is over." Why the students respected him so or why the faculty treated him with such high regard remained perplexing. He was old fashioned and frumpy, a cliché. Clichés posing as people were everywhere, surrounding her, intermingling in her circles. It was exhausting.

FIVE

The brief memorial service at the funeral home, starting the day hours before, dissipated into a blur in Henry's mind. A bevy of people showed up to pay respects to a woman they barely knew. Co-workers from the university, dressed for their workday, came, and went. Priscilla Harris-Hunt had even donned a black dress and made an appearance. A few of Henry's long-term clients awkwardly offered regrets.

It was a bizarre ceremony; paying tribute to the life and passing of the artistic woman with whom he shared everything. A tender wife of thirty years, a loving mother of their only child, and doting grandmother of the light in their lives. Her favorite music had softly filled in the unpleasant silences of the dimly lit funeral parlor. Her striking beauty looked out from an enlarged picture taken of her twenty-five years earlier, positioned near the casket. Exquisite flowers arrived that would have delighted her in life but now would be given away to strangers willing to water them.

The sacrament at the church was familiar with deep ritual and dismal organ chords. Henry drifted along during the prayers, mildly aware of the words or intent. Some long-distance cousins attended next to former students of the professor, none of whom had ever spoken to Marie. After the church service, one or two genuine friends gathered to pay respects to those left behind. Several of her former music students, now grown, offered their fond memories of her teaching techniques. Their words were bittersweet.

Miss Nadia, Marie's caregiver, squeezed Henry's hand without mouthing a word. The lump in his throat grew larger. It was all an unbearable custom.

Now he sat in a moderately stuffed, high back chair the color of ocean blue, as small groups of people chatted in corners a few feet away. Here at his daughter, Anelia's, home he had always felt comfortable, even though he rarely had the opportunity to visit over the last several years. Today there wasn't a chair on earth that could comfort him. Son-in-law Josef and grandson Dimitri busied themselves in the kitchen preparing sandwiches for the overflow of relatives, neighbors, and friends who ambled over after the observances and eventually assembled with the family.

This modest home always offered cheer no matter what the occasion. Today's circumstances, however, were somber. Well intentioned condolences were murmured, and Henry graciously acknowledged each with poise. When uninterrupted, his eyes tilted downward, and he concentrated on the memories of sweet times that replayed above the boards on the floor. Almost effortless sounds of piano chords echoed in his head accompanied by the mirthful voice of a beautiful Polish girl that he loved his whole life. Alzheimer's disease had stolen her voice, her body, her soul, but left the cherished images in Henry's mind.

They achingly reran for him as he sat engulfed by grief.

Neela, the pet name Henry tagged on his only child when she was a sprite, witnessed her mother deteriorate over time and her own reserve of strength must have grown for this eventuality. Now she appeared more concerned for the man left behind, alone, saddened, and heartbroken. She gently prodded, "Papa, let me get you a plate." Anelia's words were soft.

"No, thank you. I'm not hungry." Henry raised his tired eyes to meet hers and patted her slender, elegant, fingers. Holding her hand in his own made his recollections fly to the endless music lessons his wife taught to their daughter. How accomplished Neela had grown. The hands of a pianist…he patted her once more. His own hands sought and found the armrests where they resumed their resigned position. This blow laid him low and he had neither the inclination nor the strength to pretend he felt fine.

Six-year-old Dimitri Tomasz Ecktell and his father, Josef, exited the kitchen each with a tray of sandwiches intended to be placed on the dining room table near the vegetables and cookies. Balancing ever so well until the final steps, Dimitri tipped his tray allowing three hand crafted sandwiches to slide to the floor.

"Don't worry, Dimi, it's okay," Josef assured his son. He swiftly set down his tray to assist the boy. Dimitri's eyes filled with tears of uncertain origin. Was it the pressure of the bereavement atmosphere or his failure at the task? Could it be the stress he sensed in those closest to him? His head dropped until his chin nearly rested on his chest. On one knee, at eye level, Josef held his son. When his father's embrace loosened, Dimitri walked over to his grandfather, silently crawled onto his lap, and laid his head on the sad man's shoulder. Both felt immediate relief.

Josef stood, smiled, and returned the trays with toppled food to the kitchen. There he found his wife wiping her eyes. Quietly and briefly, they embraced with a tight hold as if to ward off the outside world of trouble and sorrow.

"There's so much for him," Anelia said to her husband. "The funeral expenses, past due payments, the empty apartment…" Her voice was urgent. "Just look at him. He's exhausted and I'm so worried about him."

Josef held on and comforted her with his embrace. What more could he do? What more could any of them do? It was going to be a day-by-day struggle.

Guests offered condolences with the usual well-meaning phrases that so often grated the bereaved more than comforted. People tried to soothe the sorrow but so often Henry's role reversed, and he consoled those in front of him. When a relative offered, "She's in a better place," he wanted to shout out his disagreement. Instead, he restrained himself and just accepted the exchange. Suffering blow after blow of negligent comments, he eventually retreated and no longer even attempted to feign appreciation.

"Would you like to lie down, Papa?" Anelia asked him as she bent close to his face.

"No, Neela. I'm okay." He reached around his grandson and patted her hand. "Dimi and I are just fine here." He hugged the child close to his chest. Dimitri resettled but made no move to leave his grampa's lap. The two stayed there for the rest of the afternoon, avoiding conversation with the well-wishers, and feeling content in their grief.

Friends and relatives had sauntered in and out of the melancholy mood inside the small home, met by the misery that was thick within each wall. People chatted, ate, remembered, cried, smiled, and eventually left.

Marie's older brother, Ted, had driven from Pittsburgh for the funeral. The last time he had seen his younger sister she was healthy and energetic. Even though Henry spoke to him a few times over recent years, the shock of her death had been hard on the man. He made the trip alone, having lost his own wife many years before to cancer. He had spoken few words, but embraced the family, each with a tight clench, squeezing their life into himself with old arms. Now, he sat in the kitchen. Attempts to console him were unsuccessful and he simply wanted to retreat into his memories. He left early for his hotel and planned to drive back to Pennsylvania the following day.

Out the window, Henry watched the gloom of grayness shift into dusk. A bit of sense urged him to make his way home where this day could be put behind him. Dimi had fallen into carefree sleep on his lap, so he motioned for Neela to come and scoop him up. Henry waited while she got him settled into bed. He thanked Josef for fixing a container of food to take home. Finally, a hug for Neela, a handshake for Josef, promises to call, and he was out the door. He felt relieved to be on his way home even though nothing about home was going to be the same. Perhaps the familiarity of the surroundings, the books on the shelves, or the toaster on the counter would reassure him.

Instead, when he entered the quiet apartment, he found himself moving toward the small bedroom that he had used by himself for the last three years. He passed the old-fashioned dresser and bed and opened the closet door before looking at the clothing hung inside. His hesitant hand reached toward the fabrics, gently feeling their softness, smoothness, or delicate texture. Through weary eyes he saw his vibrant wife wearing each article, smiling, living, and breathing within their threads. These were not what he sought. He viewed the materials for a brief time before stepping back and slowly closing the door, saving her wardrobe within. Henry moved toward the dresser and opened the middle drawer where neatly folded nightgowns laid. He chose a particularly favorite flannel piece with faded pink moons and stars and gently lifted it to his face. He smelled the fabric, the soap, the delicate skin of his wife and he lingered there, recognizing this was what he needed.

Still reverently holding the garment, he walked to the converted living room where the hospital bed remained at the center. Henry slipped out of his shoes and climbed up onto the bed. He held the nightgown as if he held Marie inside it. With the collar against his cheek, and his arms around the rest, he let his head meet the pillow. Tears filled his eyes and his hands trembled. With each breath he smelled her sweet hair, felt her young hand, saw her gentle eyes, heard her voice sing again, and the memories of their life were relived. Content that he had captured a piece of their past happiness, he relaxed, and eventually sleep overtook the pain.

SIX

Jamison Corlander tread the lavish stone pathway to the entrance of the gorgeous stucco mansion with trepidation in his belly and ideas he could not admit. The past few weeks had been confusing, but he would be lying if he said he wasn't excited. At first, the awkward meetings with his professor made him edgy. Still, she had a way of simultaneously relaxing him and intriguing him. She didn't seem to be uncomfortable, as if working so close with a student was as normal as grading research papers. His concentration drifted when he worked on assignments and when he drove to or from daily football practice. He had to shake the nasty ideas out of his head when the scent of her mind-altering perfume teased his memory. At times he was sure he was crazy and other times he wanted to follow the basic drives that emerged when his mind charged into wild vignettes.

Extensive solar lighting enhanced the lush shrubbery and gloriously colorful flowers that adorned the expansive front yard and the stone walkway. Mature trees and a sculptured hedge secluded the home from neighbors on either side. This high-end community sheltered affluent owners where professional salaries and family trusts covered a multitude of indiscretions. The antique brass fixture above the curved entry emanated a golden glow to both sides of the massive front door. Jamison heard the bell chime inside when he touched the oval button and excruciating moments passed before the heavy door opened.

Priscilla Harris-Hunt swung the great wooden door wide and greeted him with an inviting smile. She wore a subtle pink cashmere sweater and matching leggings that revealed her defined calves. Her make-up was a combination natural look and sultry eyes that complemented her shoulder length, strawberry blonde, hair, worn loose and casual rather than up like when at the university. Her earrings were small and delicate silver hoops that caught and teased a curl when she moved. She appeared youthful and athletic and smelled of that intoxicating perfume, promising intimate secrets, that she wore so effectively.

"Come in, Jamison. I'm glad you found the house." She gestured for him to enter and he did so with a jerky start and stop motion, as if he had never stepped over a threshold before, as if his own legs were hesitant, as if it were a point from which there was no turning back. He had never trodden over a boundary like this and it meant more than just a step. He had fought the idea for two days since his professor suggested they meet at her house to discuss his paper. Sometimes he didn't want to think of himself as being led into it. Other times he couldn't imagine she could be interested in him. Still other times he told himself he was an idiot. Now, the arguments were braided together. He stared at her as she walked in front of him, showing him into the living room. His heart charged within his chest. His eyes focused on her bum as she moved.

There was an intimate glow from the huge stone fireplace and an intriguing painting poised on the mantle next to an ivory sculpture. Wood lay stacked in an authentic Mongolian copper vessel on the hearth, and a few candles flickered on a marble sideboard. Jamison remained oblivious to the magnificence around him. The blue folder with his research paper rested on a glass coffee table in the center of the elegant room. He walked over near it and waited.

"Please, sit. Get comfortable." Priscilla told him. He wasn't sure it was possible. "I know you're in training, but would you like something to drink? A small glass of wine? A cocktail? I'm having one. Do you think one would hurt you?" She smiled at him with a wistful look that suggested it was okay.

It was true that he was in training, but he had always been in training. His life revolved around football. It had gotten him noticed in high school and helped get him into college. He expected that to succeed, it would be through athleticism. Hence, his struggle with the academic side of his life. It was true that there were a handful of times that he shared beers with buddies and his gridiron efforts hadn't suffered. Making it a common ritual though was out of the question. *One drink probably wouldn't hurt...*

"No thanks, ma'am," he finally said.

"Okay, no problem."

She indicated for Jamison to be seated then sat near him on the custom-made sofa. She picked up the blue folder and opened it. He settled back against the cushion and she slowly did likewise. She gestured about one line after another.

"This part here tells me that you did relevant research. And I like how you brought in the data to back up your statements in your final summary."

Jamison's stomach relaxed and he nodded in agreement. An easy tone emerged as he indicated appreciation of her professional assessment. She continued for a few moments, pointing out his aptitude and emphasizing his intelligence.

"Tell me a little about you," she said, closing the folder. She posed her body to face him as if rapt with interest in his response. A wisp of her hair curled around one shiny earring.

"Excuse me?" The juicy notions in his mind resulted in his mouth being dry as a kicker's tee.

"Where did you grow up? First girlfriend. First kiss."

"I grew up in Radford. It's a small town, not much going on." He licked his lips with a waterless tongue.

"Did you play football in high school?"

"Yes, ma'am. My dad played, then my brother and me and it was always in my blood, ya' know."

"Please, you don't have to call me ma'am. When we're alone call me Cilla, like the rest of my friends. What do your friends call you?"

"Yes, ma'am. Well, I have all kinds of names." He laughed for the first time.

"What are they?"

"Um, my mom calls me Jami, but she is the *only* one. My dad calls me 'Son' and I'm not even sure if it's from Jamison or just cuz I'm his son, ya know."

"Your buddies, what do they call you?"

"My friends from school always called me 'Cor' for the most part." His abs relaxed.

"And the girls, what do the girls call you?" She looked at him with her chin tilted so her eyes had to widen.

"Ah, well, I guess I only really had one girlfriend and that was back in high school. Football was my focus, ya know." He shifted his weight, remembering the awkward time in school when he and Maura discovered the wonders of the world. "I called her 'M' and she called me 'my man.' Silly."

"Not silly at all, overly sweet. When two people are drawn to each other it can be extremely strong. Your first love sort of sets the stage for the next one, don't you think? I mean you know what you want. You know what you don't like. You know how to do things you didn't know before." Her voice sounded like a glossy whisper. "I think I'll have my drink now. Sure, you won't join me?" She brushed against his leg as she rose. At a side table she opened a bottle of imported Chopin Vodka, and without waiting for an answer, poured two glasses. Stirring in the tonic ever so precisely, she moved toward the sofa, handed a glass to Jamison, and took a sip while she stood in front of him. "Mm, very good, what do you think?"

Jamison sipped his drink, swallowed hard, and set the glass on the table next to his blue folder.

"Good."

Priscilla lowered herself onto the sofa, lifted her left arm to the top of the cushion and edged herself toward him even closer than before.

"You are a talented young man. Your paper shows a lot of insight and reflects a considerable amount of work in its organization. I have also heard about your athletic ability. I would love to see you play. I'll bet you're like a force. So strong…"

He didn't speak. He couldn't speak.

"The clash of the teams, the individuals fighting to the goal…it's so primal…kind of sexy. What do you think?" She waited. "Do you think football is sexy, Jamison?" With that she reached for both glasses and handed his to him. She clinked his glass and peered at him over the rim as she sipped her drink. He gulped the vodka. She lightly patted the top of his thigh.

"You have to admit, it's sexy, right?" Priscilla laughed and fell against the back-cushion landing against Jamison's arm. There was nothing as dangerous as the velvet tone of a rich woman's laugh.

"Oh, sorry." She caught his eyes with hers. "Not really," she whispered. "I can't lie to you; I'm feeling something really intense right now." Her gaze was locked on him and she leaned in a little closer. "Do you feel it? My heart is racing."

Priscilla slipped her soft hand to where his bigger, stronger, hand rested and took his fingers into her grasp. She placed his palm against her breast as if to let him test her beating heart. Still peering deep into his dark eyes, she stopped talking. She took his same hand and stroked her cheek before wrapping it behind her. She raised her own fingers and stroked the skin of his sun-tanned face. She touched his magnificent ink-black hair and twisted a bit of his longish style inside her hand; all the time holding the unwavering contact in their eyes.

Finally, the masculine parts in him responded. The firm hand at her waist drew her closer and the gentle hand that had stroked her face slipped up the back of her neck and filled itself with her silky tresses. He bent his face above hers with his breath now coming in heavy bursts. She waited. His warm lips parted and gently brushed against hers. He kissed her tenderly, slowly. Her needy hands climbed over his powerful arms, squeezing his taut muscles under the shirt. Higher they rose until she wrapped around his solid shoulders and folded herself into his embrace. In another moment he was kissing her full on. His earnest lips touched hers, her cheeks, her elegant neck, and back to her mouth where his tongue plunged until he tasted her tongue in response.

His hands lightly roamed her small back, her breasts, and her arms. She pulled his woven shirt from his jeans and unbuttoned the buttons with swift eagerness. He paused long enough to slip his arms from the sleeves and Priscilla took the opportunity to shed her cashmere sweater. Displaying her ample cleavage, she stood slowly but still leaned close to the young man's face. She took both his hands and directed him to the waistband of her pink leggings indicating what she wanted. With a deliberate lingering trace, he lowered them slowly. She stepped out of each leg with a dancer's grace and a harlot's talent.

Standing before him in seductive French lingerie, she took her time looking over his bare chest and feeling his steady touch caress her legs and ass. A tiny gasp of air escaped her lips when Jamison stood up in front of her and pulled her to his warm, hard body. He took charge of the moment and assumed the alpha role. A weakness in her knees that she had not known for years zapped her strength. She stopped trying to be seductive and just held on.

"The bedroom," she whispered.

Jamison picked her up and walked out of the living room, effortlessly carrying her in the direction she pointed. He didn't notice more flickering candles in the room or the soft music that had been playing since he arrived. He didn't notice the expensive duvet cover or even the cool satin sheets that waited. He stood Priscilla up next to the bed then, with hands on her shoulders, he nudged her to sit. There, as she watched, he loosened his pants and let them fall, shed his boxers, and exposed himself, faded scars and gridiron wounds, no mistaking his manly intention.

She backed onto the bed and he crawled up after her. He took his time. Kissing, caressing, and teasing her skin into sensation. His hands were familiar with a woman's body, and he pleasured her with equal parts anticipation and satisfaction.

She used her own methods to tempt and delight; a lick, a bite, a warm fingertip over a healed injury. The familiar pleasures and new sexual experiences combined to entangle the two lovers. By morning they were no longer student and professor. They were male and female, peers despite age, embarking on an affair of mutual satisfaction. Jamison found a sense of maturity beyond his twenty-three years, afforded him by his paramour. He had no idea she was thinking the ethics conference was not going to interrupt this.

SEVEN

Peter Basefield adjusted his glasses, gathered up several papers, slipped his cell phone in his pocket, pressed the message button on his desk phone, and rose from his seat. He walked out from behind his desk, exited his office, and tapped on his boss's door.

"Come in." The time on the clock told Stuart Samson who it was. "Have a seat, Peter. I'm just finishing up this response to that health care group. Take me a minute…"

Peter sat in the sturdy leather chair in front of Stuart's desk, a familiar spot. He glanced out the window; not staring at the man while he finished his work. As promised, in a short time, Stuart pressed save on his computer and gave Peter his full attention.

"The Texas excursion," Stuart asked and confirmed in one remark.

"Chairperson Sarah Applewise is finalizing plans for the trip to McAllen, Texas. The two other delegates going are William Dalton from Missouri and Ingrid Schultz from Wisconsin. There are two researchers who have written extensively regarding trauma and Ms. Applewise is meeting with committee for authorization to have them join the delegation." Mr. Samson did not comment, so Peter continued.

"Departure date is May first. Leaving from Reagan National at 10:00 a.m. arriving McAllen Miller Airport at 4:45 p.m. Hotel accommodations are arranged. The following morning, with special permission, the delegation will visit the Catholic Charities Center under the direction of the Office of Refugee Resettlement, located in Brownsville. There you'll meet the director and Hugh Gallwith, 28th District Representative, to have a brief tour of the facility. Next, on to the U.S. Border Patrol Central Processing Center. Questions can be asked by members of the group, next a tour of the facility, and finally hear a little about its accomplishments so far.

"Later that same day you will meet with border patrol agents at McAllen station, another tour, and dinner with Mr. Gallwith.

"Due to the amount that is packed into that one day, I've arranged for a late departure the following day at 1:00 p.m. I know you are accustomed to the pace, sir, but the others may not be able to keep up with you."

"Sounds good," he said while giving Peter a half smile. The other half of the smile was in Stuart's head, knowing full well that his chief of staff was cracker jack smart and thorough. Things got done efficiently.

Stuart checked his personal planner. "May first you say?" He didn't look up, his mind already onto another subject.

"Yes, sir. I have blocked the days on your calendar."

"Very good, Peter. Thank you."

"About your address to the University of Ohio ROTC tomorrow…"

"Yes, what time is that again?"

"It's at 2:00, sir. Jerrold submitted your speech for your final approval."

"Do you have it?"

"Yes, sir. Right here." Peter produced several loose sheets of paper, double-spaced, paperclipped for easy access, from his folder and placed them on the desk. As soon as Stuart picked them up and looked them over, red pen in hand, it was clear that the other items on Peter's agenda were going to have to wait.

Having learned to read his boss's method of operation and 'do it now' approach, Peter stood up and let himself out of the room. He settled in behind his own desk and a low rumbling of his stomach made him turn his head to the watch on his wrist. It was 1:18 p.m. and he had not eaten anything since his muffin and cup of coffee before leaving home at 5:45 a.m. The desk phone rang.

More rumbling when he reached to pick up the receiver. "Office of Representative Stuart Samson."

"My name is Josef Ecktell. I'm with the Youth Service Opportunities Project returning a call to Mr. Samson."

"What is this in regard to?"

"Regarding the NPO lobbyist meeting last month." He waited.

Stuart didn't like lobbyists and held them in minor distrust. Peter inherited similar opinions through osmosis. "Please wait, while I check to see if he is in." With that, he pressed the hold button.

"It's Josef Ecktell from YSOP. Says he's returning your call." Many people used the ploy in bygone days to get connected with the congressman. Peter waited through the silence on the other end as his hunger resumed.

"Put him through."

Indeed, Stuart had expected to hear from Mr. Ecktell. At a previous meeting, the younger man stood out as intelligent and genuine. They exchanged a few words and Stuart had given him his business card. The first impression had been more urgent at the time of the meeting. Now, with the disadvantage of elapsed time, Stuart was distracted by more pressing political events. He mustered up a congenial tone.

"Josef, nice to hear from you." Stuart reached for some documents to slide into a folder and grabbed his bottle of water.

"Thank you for taking my call. I appreciate your busy schedule so I will keep this brief. At the lobbyist meeting a month ago you and I spoke about the Youth Services Opportunities Project that I am affiliated with and at the time you were interested in it. Since we met, I've compiled some stats and created a small spreadsheet with information of how this could impact your campaign in your home state of Ohio. Knowing that you have a year left in your current term, I imagine you will be taking to the campaign trail soon and this would be a great lead in for your platform targeting young voters."

Even the best politicians had to be re-elected to be effective. Some of Stuart's distraction had been about his upcoming bid. He had served a year of his third term and felt confident about his chances but there always loomed the possibility of a shiny fresh contender. It was never far from his consciousness to place himself in a favorable light. This youth program was not just polished on the surface. Voters would be impressed with the outcome statistics he had already seen. Positive results appealed to him and he was hopeful his constituents would agree. His interest was vaguely stolen away from his cluttered desk.

"Go on," he said.

"Your base is solid, Congressman. In your last run for re-election, you focused on the young voters in your state and it comprised seventy-five percent of your efforts. To keep those votes, and to provide consistency, it is my belief that affiliating yourself with YSOP could help solidify this next election's hub. Your focal point has been to appeal to the young people, the grass roots of society. I'm offering you the chance to connect with YSOP of Washington, D.C., branch out to Dayton, and Akron in your home state. Young voters will again get on board. Established voters, parents, educators, employers, will also see the benefits involved. Those constituents are in a position to appreciate the work done by the NP." Josef didn't talk too much or too fast. He allowed a pause for Stuart to absorb his words.

Besides youthful voters, Stuart's campaign espoused issues that included the separation of children and parents at the U.S., Mexican border. This pressing subject had appealed to him on a personal level. It gripped him in a way that tweaked his conscience and needled his morality.

"You have done your homework, Josef." The planner on his desk indicated three meetings that afternoon. "Why do I need you to 'set me up' with YSOP when you know I can make contact with them directly?" Now he was rummaging through the drawer for his USB thumb drive.

"Stuart, this is what I do. The luncheons, the meetings, the introductions, the call backs…it can all be taken out of the hands of your office. You're busy. Your aides are busy. Let me get rolling on this and run some ideas by you in a few days."

"I *am* busy." It was a statement that he made as he stood up with briefcase in hand.

"It's a 'yes' then?" Josef asked.

"Okay, get back with my staff chief, Peter, to set up a meeting between you and me in a few days. Impress me." *Again.* He hung up the phone moving toward the door. For a second, he let his beliefs hover over the idea of the Youth Services Opportunities Project and the fact he honestly did endorse what they stood for. He checked his back pocket to see his wallet still held its place.

EIGHT

Josef expected that Peter Basefield blocked out thirty minutes to meet with his boss. He understood that congressmen didn't like to admit that they sometimes needed lobbyists. Josef respected Representative Samson and his prior research assured him that there was a definite niche the YSOP could fill to mutual gain. His strategy was to be congenial, professional, and to the point. He thanked Peter Basefield and entered the congressman's small office ready to pitch.

"Josef, nice to see you again." The robust man stood up, promptly came around his desk, and extended his hand. He motioned for Josef to sit, while returning to his modest chair.

"Thank you for seeing me, Congressman. I will be conscious of your time." And so, the summary of the Youth Services Operations Project origin, details, and successes rolled off Josef's tongue with ease and pride. The element of Stuart's involvement and mutual benefit came across as an advantage in an election campaign just as Josef had intended. He offered statistics and a spreadsheet but did not belabor the individual features. He sensed Stuart's favorable attention, so he leaned forward to establish a commitment. "There are some planned activities the first week of May that you might be interested in attending, sir. It could be the kickoff of your affiliation."

"Can't do the beginning of May. Going to be in Texas."

"Oh, Texas."

"I have a delegation going to look at the situation at the border."

Josef paused for an appropriate response. "It's quite the dilemma."

"Yes."

"I'm sure you will use your platform to the best possible outcome."

"Mm."

"My father-in-law speaks of the separation there from time to time. It worries him." Josef measured his words. He didn't see Stuart turn his eyes directly to him.

"What does your father-in-law do?"

"He is a professor at the University of Virginia. He teaches several post-grad and doctorate level Psychology classes. He also counsels families who have experienced trauma in his private practice. I believe he grasps the immigration predicament because he also came from another country when he was a child. It's a soft spot."

"Has he ever discussed his experience?" Stuart slipped off his glasses and leaned back in his chair.

By now, the time slot that Josef had imagined he had been penciled into had elapsed. The question drew a personal connection and Josef chose his words prudently. "He spoke to me about it once. Didn't dwell on the experience. Made me know it was something I wanted to remember."

"Can you talk about it?"

"My father-in-law's name is Henry Novak. He lived with his family in a city in Poland. It's a hard name to pronounce and you shouldn't even attempt to spell it." His dimples deepened when he smiled. "At that point there were his parents, an older sister, and a younger sister. The city was on the Polish border of Ukraine and Czechoslovakia. He would laugh that depending on who occupied Poland at the time, the inhabitants were Polish one day and something else the next. His father was a cooper."

"He made barrels?" Stuart asked.

"Yes. Wine, ale, that sort of barrel. Money was always stretched thin with the growing family. Eventually, his father traveled alone to the U.S. to find a good job in the land of opportunity. It took two years for him to be able to send for his wife and children. The severance was difficult for the little ones. It was a grim time for the whole family.

"Henry told me about the ship that brought them over. The state rooms on board were small. The waves rocked the boat. The food was strange. It took two weeks to get to the east coast. Lots of people were sick and his younger sister grew weak over time." Josef noticed Stuart nod as he explained what he had heard only once, the night his own son was born.

"Coming off the ship there was a narrow wooden plank where passengers had to cross stretching from the vessel to the dock. My father-in-law's family was caught up in the hustle to disembark. The older sister, about six, I think, went first. Next Henry's mother carried the youngest in her arms. Henry followed, holding on to his mother's skirt. Henry said he stumbled and fell on the plank while crossing over. He described seeing the deep water beneath him, black and choppy. He was terrified. The sight and the feeling never left him. The night he told me this, he said he still gets chills at the memory, sixty some years later." Josef readjusted his tie and shuffled his feet with the retelling of the story. So much risk and peril were involved in the decision to set out on the desperate voyage.

"My wife is an immigrant," Stuart confided. "Her family arrived from Astana, Kazakhstan at a time when refugees from the former Soviet Republic were questionably regarded. Her description of the brave journey and cold reception prompted me to always try to educate and inform others in government at every opportunity."

Stuart met his wife, Inzhu, in college after her family immigrated to the U.S. At the time her family sought citizenship, Kazakhstan had a large Islamic population, affiliations with China and Russia, and was a questionable immigration risk. Talk of the discrimination and red tape that abounded during their courtship could make his jaw tighten.

"I didn't know."

"Your father-in-law sounds like a special man." Stuart was still looking at Josef.

"He is sir. I can assure you."

"He works with families who have experienced trauma?"

"Yes. He has a private practice, and he has been in the field for thirty-plus years."

"Well, I'd like to meet him one day. In the meantime, please stop at Peter's desk and arrange a time when we can formally begin our YSOP affiliation."

"Thank you so much, Congressman." Josef reached to shake the man's hand.

He stepped outside the office and silently acknowledged the man was all the positive things he expected him to be.

Peter Basefield was already looking at a screen with highlighted areas in red, yellow, blue, and green, indicating meetings, lunches, activities, and fundraisers. Josef stopped at the desk and removed his own iPad to sync dates.

NINE

"You should do it," Anelia was saying.

"I don't know," her father stammered. His wife had been gone a few weeks and the idea of getting involved with this unusual project sounded like too much for him. He held the notepad in his hand and stared at the words he had written as he spoke to his daughter.

"A complete change of focus might be helpful. It's a short time. Less than a week. It's probably a lot warmer in Texas than here."

"Ahh," he scoffed at her attempt to convince him.

"Papa, to think that they invited you to go, it's such an honor. They must have high regard for your work, teaching, and counseling. It's amazing. Mama would be so proud."

It didn't take much for Henry to consider how his wife might react since his focus rarely strayed from her memory. Yes, she would be proud. He lived his whole life hoping to make her proud of him as he was of her. It would bring her a smile to know of this opportunity. What a joy it would be to see that smile again. His mind wandered off to happier days. He forgot the cell phone until his daughter spoke again.

"Papa, just take some time, think about it before you decide. You can do that much."

Henry had a mixture of psychology classes to teach at the University of Virginia. He had several families to counsel in his private practice. Rearranging his schedule was not without complications. This congressional delegation was leaving in May, just two weeks out.

The dedication he felt for the students and clients had truthfully waned a bit since the death of his wife. It was not to say that he no longer cared about them, it was more like he cared a little less about everything. If he was being honest, he wasn't sure he had the energy to go to D.C., let alone Texas. He recognized the symptoms of depression in himself, but he rationalized his grief was normal. Medical expenses, funeral expenses, a month of wages for Miss Nadia, and a looming pharmacy tab nagged at him until his chest sunk. For a moment, his interest over participation in the brief excursion peaked, but fell off once more.

"When Josef got the call from Representative Samson, the man said he really hoped you would accept his invitation. Someone else had to drop out and he remembered that Josef talked about your trauma work. He hoped you might find the situation interesting and be able to offer insight with your background and experience.

"By the way, Josef feels the same as I do, just so you know. I realize that you respect his opinion, so I'll let you talk to him again if you like." He was aware she was playing every card she could in order to convince him to get back on the track of living life again. *Hadn't it occurred to her that he just might know what was best for himself.*

"I'm going to call the number and talk to Mr. Samson, but I'm not promising anything. Now go take care of my grandson and stop badgering me." He clicked off the phone with a sigh of relief to have the conversation over.

The notes were in front of him. He looked closely once more at the words Josef had told him. A combination of pride and apprehension blossomed at the same time.

"Matka, what do you think?" He laid the pad on the table and scuffed across the floor into the kitchen for a hot cup of tea.

The flattering idea of being invited kept creeping into his contemplations but disbelief would wash right over. He could hardly imagine himself with such an honor in such important company. He glanced at the details which increased the weight on his shoulders. The timing was unfortunate. It was too soon after Marie's death. There was so little time to decide.

"Tell me what to do," he said out loud, rubbing his forehead. As if his wife were in the next room, he heard her say, "*Of course, you'll go. Who better than you?*"

"Oh, Matka. You don't know how tired I feel." His head rested in his hand as he spoke. "If only you were with me." He heard, "*I am.*"

He didn't understand the whirlwind that was taking control of his life. Some days he didn't feel like himself, more like a shell, a robot, moving without purpose. Now, that feeling engulfed him, and he acted without intention. Doing what she would have wanted was the motivation that kept him alive. Little more than that had any influence at all.

A burdened sigh escaped his lungs followed by another. He didn't want to rise from the chair. He didn't want to take the next step. He didn't know how to live. But he would do all of it. He would call the number. He would go to Washington. He would agree.

* * *

Henry was hunched over his keyboard upon the cluttered desk at the university composing test questions based on a recent cognitive psychology lecture. His hands trembled over the keys. This day marked the first time that he had over-slept and arrived late for his morning lecture. The fact demoralized him. It was more like him to be early, prepared, and anticipatory about his lectures and students.

Lately, he felt drowsy much of the time and, if truth be known, could easily drift into a nap on the spot. His appetite had left him. He wanted nothing more than to crawl into bed and pull the covers over his head. The wrap of the blankets and the softness of the pillows were the only respite that offered comfort he could abide.

Finally, when the printer spat out the original, he had just completed, he proofread each question for validity, attached a post-it-note for fifty-five copies, and slipped it between the sides of a manila folder. A noise behind him drew his attention.

"Henry," slipped out as Priscilla Harris-Hunt entered the room and closed the door. Her suit was neat with perfect jewelry to accent the soft shade of coral in the coordinated silk blouse. Her hair was pulled away from her pretty face with its subtle make-up. Today, her heels were only two and a half inches high.

"Good afternoon, Priscilla."

"How *are* you?" A little surprise tinged her voice since he was not on the timetable for office hours.

"Well, thank you for asking. I wanted to mention something to you." He skipped the inquiry about himself. As he rearranged some of his paperwork, he picked up a class schedule and swiveled his chair to face hers. She sat down and let her detailed leather briefcase rest on her polished desktop. She half smiled before he continued.

"I have been invited to join a group of government representatives for a brief program. It requires me to be away from the university for a week. I talked to Douglas and he gave me the go ahead. Said he would have my classes covered. I mentioned to him that I would ask you to take my level four STATS group. You're the only one who knows it well enough.

It's a lot to ask, I know. Do you think you could manage?"

Priscilla looked away from his face toward her own calendar.

"I'm quite sure Douglas said he would have adjuncts and TAs for the remainder, referring to the slew of teacher assistants that professors often used. You're the only one, I think, that could take this over and pull it off on short notice."

"You're probably right about that." She looked as if she wanted to say more, but there was the fact that recently, he lost his wife.

"Sure thing, Henry. I'd be happy to help you out."

"Very good."

"I can drop in to let the department chairman know we've talked," she offered.

"I have test copies to request, so I'll tell Douglas myself when I'm down there. Thank you." Both swiveled toward their desks; Henry concentrated on papers, student notes, and telephone messages while Priscilla pulled her leather planner from her pink briefcase.

Another noise from the office entrance occurred without warning. A tall, young, Native American man knocked on the frame.

"Excuse me, Professor," he looked at Henry as he opened the door. "I didn't know you were here. I, um, was supposed to check on my research paper."

Henry didn't recognize the student from any of his classes. When Professor Harris-Hunt looked up, the young man's eyes slowly shifted toward her.

"Oh yes, Mr. Corlander. I did direct you to come to my office during this time. Dr. Novak was doing some extra work but was about to visit Chairman Yantz. Sit down." She waved the young man toward a chair.

Henry didn't speak. He didn't respond to the emphatic dismissal in her voice, just persisted in reviewing some notes. As the student sat in silence, Henry remained about his business for several more minutes before making the slightest moves toward leaving. He slipped several papers into his bag with quivering hands, glanced along his bookshelf, squinted across his desk, and stood. He headed toward the door and the hallway beyond without acknowledging his co-worker or the student.

Behind the door that Henry closed, Jamison Corlander leaned forward and turned the lock with a click. He gradually rose from the seat, his eyes still fixed on the woman's.

TEN

"Mamá, mamá," seven-year-old Mateo screamed as he reached his scrawny arms toward the ragged woman being ushered through a steel door. So many doors.

After stumbling around in darkness before dawn, the pounding in his head had blurred his vision. He remained silent about the pain after what he witnessed happening to his mother. She had also stayed quiet as they grappled with spiny cactus and clinging burrs and rusting wires that protruded amid the broken bricks and mangled roots that covered the ground. She had bruises and cuts but had relentlessly led him forward.

Haggard strangers squatted quietly by a mound of earth. Mateo thought he must look like they looked. His mother continued to trudge ahead, and he barely managed to keep up. It had been a series of disasters that went on for so long, one after another, then still another, until he lost sense of the order of events. He wanted to rest, needed to stop, and eat, but she continued, so he fought to maintain movement. The last he remembered, his knees turned to mush, and his eyes saw only a tunnel before he collapsed.

The heavy steel door that opened into the building was being held by a man with a round face, a mustache, and no lips. Mateo's thoughts were still fuzzy, but he had held his mother's hand at the end and walked under his own strength. Next there was a door that entered a tight room with a few glass partitions and a metal detector at the front. His mother passed through before him and then it was his turn. A few minutes of waiting were followed by an escort through one more door where the room was as big as his whole house back home. There were many agents in dark uniforms, and yet another door at the far end. One of the agents approached him, taking hold of both arms. His mind was as dull as his muscles. When his mother was led away, he reacted with instinctive resistance.

"Por favor, mama, vayaś no." He struggled in the grip of the border agent who restrained him and pleaded with his mother not to leave. He saw the alarm on her face, and attempted to run toward her, using all the energy that remained in his young body after the arduous journey that included unspeakable hardship. He continued to call out while his wailing and flailing proved a daunting task for the man who grappled to keep his grip on the child. Eventually, managing a bear hug for restriction, the man raised the child off the ground, and gained limited control. The boy continued to thrash about until even he understood the futility. Fear of this foreboding predicament overtook the sorrow of watching his crying mother leave. So much had already been taken from him. He pounded his fists in the direction of the agent, but only random blows landed against the arms of the man.

At last, a woman in the same uniform came up to the child and spoke in his native language. *"¿Como te llama?"* She asked his name with a temperate voice as she stood nearby. In defiance, he ignored her and wrestled with waning vigor. *"Estarás bien,"* she promised. *"Va a estar bien."* With a slow movement, she reached out toward the child and softly touched his shoulder. *"No te preocupes,"* she assured him there was no need to worry.

Hearing his language and feeling her contact caused his resistance to ease up. He squirmed for a better look at the woman who had spoken. Her eyes were not dark like his, and her skin was pale. She did not look like anyone he had known, yet her words were familiar in this strange place. He had struggled for weeks to reach the magic country where people could be safe. His tired parents promised him rest if he withstood the unending hardships of the grueling journey. He had been hungry, sick, exhausted, and afraid. They hadn't known about this last part he was certain. His parents would have prepared him. After all the disasters they had endured together this recent obstacle ripped apart the only bond that was left.

For two years, Eduardo and Rosa Elmar had scraped and planned to make the dangerous trek from San Jose Calderas in Guatemala, to the U.S. border. Now their family was separated.

ELEVEN

The day was cool with a slight wind from the east, and traffic along I-95 was fast and fierce. Josef drove this familiar route as the two men headed toward D.C. For a while, the radio provided news and traffic reports. Eventually, Josef switched off the volume and spoke to his father-in-law. "If you're worried, don't be. I know Congressman Samson and he's a good man. Did I tell you I'm working with him through YSOP?"

"About a hundred times," Henry responded without turning from the window. His voice was raspy, and he gave a vibe of irritability. With each pothole identified, he bounced and flinched like a toddler in a seat too big. A part of him was already regretting his decision. The other part of him was certain it was a bad idea.

"He's a good man. This trip will help him to shed light on the crisis. More accurate light.

"See. Henry, as a psychologist you're not political. I mean I know you have viewpoints but you're not seeking election nor endorsing a candidate. You have no agenda, just experience, having been academically trained to assess trauma, observe behavior. You may even suggest treatment for the detainees. And you, Henry, you're one of the best! Remember how you identified that case of fugue you told me about years ago? I didn't even know what fugue was until that whole thing was written up in the psych journal. And what about the kid you saved when his mother came to see you? She was the client, but you figured out the child was in danger after the first visit. You recognized the signs. Henry, this is what you do. Stuart invited *you.* They need a guy like you. You're the rock star here. You should be feeling really special about all of it." His voice was charged like a telephone pole during a lightning storm.

Henry understood that Josef was comfortable in Washington. That was his wheelhouse. He spent a lot of time with the senators and congressmen. He grasped the geography in every sense of the word. Henry respected his son-in-law and even believed most of what he said. His discomfort, however, was imbedded. There were so many questions and he doubted his presence on this delegation would make any difference with the current situation at the border. In fact, if it hadn't been for Neela's pestering, he would not be sitting in the car for this two-and-a-half-hour drive. He harrumphed.

"Yes." It wasn't an agreement; more of an appreciation that Josef had ceased talking.

One thing that Henry could feel positive about was the fact they had come a day ahead of departure. He didn't like to be rushed and wanted a chance to get his bearings and probably his courage. It was gracious for Josef to bring him. He could have taken a bus but had to admit this was better.

Halfway into the trip, traffic slowed to a crawl. Occasionally, a horn sounded as a motorist tried to forcefully merge. The unexpected sound would cause Henry to stiffen. He was not accustomed to the stress of such a commute even though he had traveled to D.C. a few previous times. Knowing that Josef was not flustered helped keep things manageable. When the reality of what he was about to do crept in, Henry would feel himself get a little warm. He remained silent, like a rock, a warm rock.

"Don't worry. Traffic gets like this. I'm kind a' used to it." Josef's words were reassuring.

The trip dragged on longer than Henry expected. Ultimately, they arrived at the Marriott at Thirteen Thirty-One Pennsylvania Avenue where Henry assumed that some of the other participants would also be staying. The hotel was tall and lavish with brick and stone rising fifteen stories. A young valet in a crisp fitting uniform smiled as he took the keys to Josef's car and gestured toward the elegant entrance.

Beyond the glass threshold, and just past reception, brilliant crystal chandeliers hung in line throughout the extended reception hall, like expensive earrings on an A-list celebrity. The hotel itself was an attraction with its glittering opulence. After checking in, they took the elevator up to their room on the fourteenth floor.

"Do ya feel like hitting the workout room?" Josef asked as he set out his razor and shave cream.

"No thanks. You go ahead." Henry responded as he hung some things in the closet.

"Maybe a dip in the pool would relax you. What do ya think?"

"I didn't bring a suit." Henry pretended to be busy pulling a few things out of his suitcase.

"Maybe a short walk to stretch your legs?"

"A little later."

Josef was genuinely unpacking and purposefully placing his things. He disappeared into the bathroom and came out in a t-shirt and gym pants.

"If I hit the treadmill are you just gonna sit here?" His question was valid.

"Maybe I'll catch the news."

"Okay. I'll be back." He was out the heavy door with a room keycard and a towel.

Henry breathed a sigh to be alone. He grabbed the TV remote and switched it on. He flipped through several stations, waiting impatiently for each one to come into view as he pressed the channel changer. The news station appeared. The topic was Chinese tariffs and the pros and cons of their effectiveness. He slogged through a dozen more channels; thumbs down to *Real Housewives, Pickers*, *Survivor* reruns, and *The View*. He switched it off and tossed the remote on his bed.

He stood in front of the room's only window, opened the floor length curtains, and parted the sheers. The view was spectacular. It provided blocks of tall buildings, a grassy mall lined with cherry blossoms, ending with the impressive Washington Monument. Henry stood awestruck.

For a moment, he remained motionless while taking in the history and relevance of where he was. The emotions emerged, inspiring and humbling, coursing through his frame. His fingers found their way to his trousers where they non-consciously slid into the pockets. His shoulders lifted a bit higher and he stood a bit taller. A reflective spirit passed through him and provided a stream of all the American memories he mustered from textbooks, moon landings, peace treaties, jet planes, and battleships. He inhaled the aura of government and change and responsibility and country…while his body filled with pride. A restless need to move overcame him. He grabbed the additional room keycard, let himself out, and proceeded down the long, carpeted hall.

On the ground floor, he passed the pool and the workout room; moving quickly so that Josef would not try to babysit him. There were spacious waiting areas furnished with tastefully overstuffed chairs and gleaming tables perfect for informal visits. Sculptures and paintings that each cost more than a month's rent, adorned the area. Henry traveled seldom, another reason the whole adventure provided a dimension of apprehension. There was a coffee niche complete with tempting smells from homemade chocolate chip cookies. Henry passed it up.

Outside of the imposing building, he wasn't sure which way to go. He was thinking of a short stroll to immerse himself in the significance of his surroundings. Maybe around the block. Clearly, the hotel *was* the block.

Lush planters displaying manicured greens and flowers were stationed to greet guests. Henry wondered what kind of flowers would be blooming around the end of April. Marie would have been able to identify each. He delighted in her explaining the differences between spring blooms such as daffodil and iris. When they walked along the city park near their home, she would brighten as she stooped to touch the delicate petals.

"*Aren't they lovely*?" He could hear her say. "*These are hyacinths. Smell them.*" She would smile at them and he would smile at her. Now a breeze chilled him, so he moved along. Left foot, right foot. Turn right at each corner. He had been correct in estimating the hotel was the entire block. He hadn't counted on the fact that there were some areas that he would be prevented from crossing. Fences with signs indicating employees only thwarted him. Other areas housed dumpsters. In the end, he doubled back and arrived at the entrance. It was peaceful standing beneath the overhang, so he remained there. The revolving door spun as guests came or went. The young valet hopped to acknowledge each.

The slight shift of daylight into evening signaled a breeze and drop in temperature, enough encouragement for him to go on inside. The path to the elevator, congested with busy people and rolling luggage, caused Henry to momentarily consider taking the stairs until reason set in. Fourteen flights would have even given Josef pause. What was he thinking at sixty-seven? Patiently, he waited until the elevator was free, pressed fourteen and watched the steel doors close from inside. Marriott didn't provide a button thirteen, nor a thirteenth floor. Back at the room he heard the shower running, confirming Josef had worked enough and called it quits.

Henry's pants rustled as he moved toward the chair he had sat in earlier. Energized by the walk, he was glad to have gotten outside and was now ready for a bit of dinner. Again, he switched on the TV and searched for news.

"Hey, is that you?" Josef called with the door slightly open.

"No." Henry replied.

"Okay. I'm thinking dinner. You hungry?" came the voice through the steam and crack in the door.

"Yes."

"Give me a minute and I'll be ready." The door closed and a few inaudible sounds emerged.

Henry was not fashion conscious about his clothes, nor did he notice what others wore. There was no point in trends or statements. It was common for him to wear what was appropriate for weather. If a sweater lasted ten years all the better. He brought a suit for the actual flight in the morning but had no intention of changing clothes now. All he had done was sit in a car and walk outside. There was no need to change from his khaki pants, blue button-down shirt, and brown sweater. They were just going to eat something, not meet the president.

Henry's deliberations were interrupted when Josef swung the bathroom door wide and stepped out in his underwear followed by a warm draft of moist air. Without looking up he pulled open a drawer and donned socks, t-shirt, and stood to pull a pair of slacks off a hanger. Next, he buttoned on a white shirt and looped a conservative striped tie. When the necktie was straight, Josef reached for his watch. At that point Henry asked, "Are you going to the same place I'm going?"

Josef gave a quiet chuckle. "That's a fair question, Henry. It must look like I'm really dressing up. But whenever I come to D.C. I'm sort of always working. In the event I run into someone I'm involved with; I want to be prepared. In my mind if I'm dressed like this, I'm on my game, ya know?"

"You look a little stiff," was Henry's observation. "We're just getting dinner."

"I'll try to stay loose. What are you hungry for?" Josef asked as he re-entered the bathroom to comb through his wavy brown hair one more time. The polished black shoes were the final touch as he checked his image in the full-length mirror. Finally, he gave his entire attention to Henry who sat slumped into the side chair and stared at him from there.

"I'm going to let the menu decide for me. Are you good looking enough yet?"

"It's all the job. Gotta' look the part. Ready?"

Henry rose from the chair and walked behind the younger man to the door. Without even a glance toward the mirror or a hand through his hair, he was ready to go. Quiet prevailed while they waited at the elevator.

Henry stood by Josef as the vault hurled them to the main floor. His tired eyes rose to the back of his son-in-law's neck and over his unbending shoulders. His right hand briefly rested on the younger man's suit. "Thanks for today."

"No problem."

TWELVE

Henry had not expected to sleep. A strange bed and a big day were just two of so many reasons he could have tossed around as he had each night for so many previous weeks. With the grace of mother earth and father sky he was able to drop into a deep and sustained rest. He roused to the sound of Josef's cell phone alarm on its third go round. Rising straight away, he got up to take first turn in the bathroom.

He shaved without a nick by repeating, *stay calm* as he stared at himself in the hotel room mirror. After a warm shower and a toweling off he wiped the mirror, sink, tub, and floor. Josef was watching news on TV when he emerged.

"Nothing new to report. Do you want this on?" Josef rose extending the remote to Henry. "I'm gonna hit the shower."

"Leave it on. I'll listen while I get dressed." He heard nothing that was said on the TV. His mind was intent on what lay ahead.

When he considered being invited to join this trip a string of neurons fired through his body. The sensation occurred often since the original phone call with Stuart Samson. He was of a mind to believe that most government officials already had the answers to the questions they were asking. That confounded him further when trying to justify his presence among the rest of the members of the consortium. What value might he add? What insight might he offer? Why was he found suitable to accompany the others? The questions in Henry's mind gave way to doubts of his competence. At that point he needed a distraction; he headed to the mirrored closet.

The dark suit was hanging where he placed it upon arrival. The feel of it prompted memories of the recent funeral. *Maybe I should get a new suit.* He could not remember if he bought this when Dimi was baptized or before. It was in the blurry pictures from that wonderful day. The smiling faces of such a happy family were filed in the "then" folder of his departmentalized brain. He wasn't ready to abandon the two-piece with its wide lapels, four-holed buttons, and sentiment just yet even if the images always surfaced when he put on this coat and pants.

He gave in to the full-length reflection of himself and straightened his gray and burgundy striped tie. He placed a fresh hankie in his pocket and slid his thin leather wallet into his pants. The wedding ring on his left hand never came off so he didn't need to hunt for it. It appeared he was ready. Josef himself wore a dark suit and tie and was set to leave the room.

The pair made their way to the main floor where Henry observed the hustle and bustle of a D.C. morning. Guests dressed in business clothes were coming and going in a reserved rush. No one ambled. Each appeared filled with a determined destination. Some of the importance found its way to Henry's shoes and seeped into his feet as he shifted weight from one to the other. A realization enveloped him that he was also an important individual on this day, about to join a congressman and others. His shoulders squared again as they had the night before when the grandeur of the area became obvious to him. Now he felt the slightest thread that he was deserving to be where he was. The feeling was fleeting.

"Breakfast is served over here." Josef led the way to the twenty-four-foot buffet. Despite the early hour, there were several guests already eating or filling their plates. Henry observed the lay of the land. There were scrambled eggs mixed with green peppers under a metal dome, bacon and sausages under another, hash browns and country fries beneath a third. A dozen flavors of yogurt lay in a bed of ice next to a display of cereals. Bagels and a variety of breads were housed behind a plexiglass container side-by-side with small muffins and cinnamon buns with icing. Large silver bowls of fruit, domestic and exotic, were being depleted by tongs grabbing at the choices. Juices were readily available at the end of the station. A chef, outfitted in a starched white uniform with matching toque, stood at the ready to prepare custom omelets.

Josef picked up a warm plate, silver utensils, a linen napkin, and headed to one end of the food display. He filled his plate with small portions and scoured the room for an available place to sit. Henry followed him with a cup of coffee in his hand.

"Aren't you going to eat?"

"Yes, but not yet. I think coffee first."

"We'll have to leave shortly, to get to the airport on time. Can't depend on traffic to be cooperative." It was a cautionary comment as well as a countdown.

"How do people drive in this urgency every day?" Henry was wondering more about the general rush. Rush of traffic with cars, buses, taxis, but also schedules, agendas, airports, buffets, lives. The incessant rush was more evident to him lately; or was it that his pace had tottered. People were moving so fast, seemingly to important destinations. Where were they going? Momentarily, he recalled the story with Holden Caulfield asking the perpetual question, 'where do the ducks go?' Was he the same now; asking where he was supposed to go?

And then they were in a taxi, then in an airport, and then Henry was on a plane sitting next to a man with thick graying eyebrows holding an empty pipe.

* * *

Once people had found their appointed rooms in the hotel, there was a built-in interval to rest and refresh. Afterward, the six individuals found their way to the lobby and agreed on the growing hunger among them. Anticipation morphed into trepidation over the promised *real* Mexican dinner they were about to enjoy. By the time they were seated in the side room of the restaurant the clock showed after 7:00 p.m.

A dark-haired woman in her thirties brought out chips and placed a bowl of queso, a bowl of red salsa, and a bowl of green salsa to the left of every other guest. People ordered drinks and the server wrote dinner requests while chewing gum at a ludicrous speed. Chips flew into the dips and into mouths.

There was an ease of manner as Stuart Samson sat in his chair, straight yet casually. He spoke with confidence, looking into the gathering, making easy eye contact.

"Corny as this may sound, I'd like to go around the table and have you say a word about yourselves and your backgrounds as a means of introduction. Please indulge me." He nodded with a grin toward the woman on his right to start off the round.

Sarah Applewise introduced herself as Chairman of the Immigration Oversight Committee. Her brown hair was fashioned after Dorothy Hamill and her slacks and soft sweater were a matching pale mauve.

"My education includes a doctorate in education administration and a juris doctorate in law. I have been an advocate for teachers and schools, and my comprehension of the legal system provides insight into needs of organizational policy. My interest in the placement of refugee children has been a catalyst during my time in Washington." Sarah smiled toward Stuart. Her introduction underscored her experience, and her voice was gently reassuring. As an afterthought, she offered in a modest tone, "Might I add that I have a tween-age daughter who consistently refreshes my understanding, or lack thereof, about the needs of the young sect."

William Dalton was in the dining chair right of Sarah. His robust voice was easy to hear above the chewing and sipping. He was six feet three inches tall and still looked like an athlete at almost fifty years of age. His brown hair was tinged with gray and his pale blue eyes sparkled with what could only be described as intellectual curiosity. Looking at his boyish face could only hint at the brainpower behind his affable smile.

"I'm House Representative Will Dalton from the great state of Missouri," he boomed. "My history includes many, many years of public service beginning with college days at the University of Missouri. I volunteered with no less than ten student organizations, formed three long-term community improvement projects, instigated a campus environmental alliance each year I attended the university, and played football all four years. No matter what anyone may tell you, sports discipline helps when you're in politics. I'm just sayin'." There was polite laughter along with a yelp from someone who had inadvertently dipped into the green salsa.

"Ms. Ingrid Schultz," Stuart stated her name and gestured toward the light-haired woman seated next to Will, "has been a representative from Wisconsin for nearly sixteen years."

With only the hint of a German accent, she talked about her education beginning in Berlin, where she grew up, and culminating at the University of Wisconsin where she achieved doctoral degrees in higher education and developmental child psychology.

"I launched my professorship in Madison where I ended up chairing the psych department. I've enjoyed a long-term affiliation with Catholic Charities and its service and outreach program.

"Several of the children who have been separated from parents, are currently being looked after until legal matters are sorted out and immigration status is decided. They are placed in caring facilities which receive financial support through the Office of Refugee Resettlement." Her voice was compelling, as one familiar with intricate details on the subject.

Stuart nodded to the distinguished man with bushy eyebrows and the ever-present cherrywood sitter pipe.

"My name is Zigmund Zellovitch. I have some familiarity with trauma."

Stuart Samson filled in the blanks. "Dr. Zellovitch is an accomplished trauma researcher at Columbia University, having published extensively in the American Journal of Psychiatry and the Journal of Traumatic Stress. Presently, he teaches courses of advanced neuro-cognitive functioning and bio-psycho-social behavioral responses to trauma, while continuing his research. We are thrilled that he has agreed to be part of this small excursion." Zigmund raised his pipe as a fair salute.

Henry was the last to speak after having heard the others' impressive accomplishments. The plate in front of him with remaining refried beans didn't seem to provide any assistance in forming a narrative.

"I'm Henry Novak. I'm an educator in the psychology program at the University of Virginia. I have a private practice counseling individuals and families who have experienced trauma."

"Henry, you're too modest. I understand you've held your position at the university for thirty years and your private practice is what, twenty years and counting? You have several published research papers, and your experience is invaluable. We're delighted you could be here." Stuart's genuine enthusiasm reassured Henry.

Stuart pushed his plate forward and dabbed his lips with the red cloth napkin. His remarks were written, yet he need not refer to them. This project was significant enough that he could speak from memory. At times it sounded as if he spoke from his heart.

"I'm happy to be in the company of this exceptional group of accomplished and diverse professionals. A few short months ago I was honored with the appointment to a committee concerned with immigration. Unabashedly, I made a nuisance of myself until my colleague, Sarah Applewise here agreed to assemble this delegation. Our small group is having the privilege of visiting some important sites involved in the immigration process. Whether our inclination is to agree or disagree with the current practice of separation, there are legitimate arguments regarding the nature of the rule.

"Many of us may not realize that similar policies in one form or another have been in effect for the last twenty years. Immigration guidelines were enforced by the former three presidential administrations. Our group is not the first to make a visit like this and certainly won't be the last. I admit to having a personal interest in the immigration situation, but other significant organizations are, and have been continuously, calling for action. Amnesty International and K.I.N.D., kids in need of defense, a nonprofit, advocating for unaccompanied minors, are just two of many.

"We'll be visiting a refugee center. This particular one run by Catholic Charities, but there are also Jewish sponsored locations, and others, for example. These child immigrant sites are funded by the government Office of Refugee Resettlement under the umbrella of Health and Human Services." Stuart slid off his glasses and placed them on the table next to his plate. "It seems as if the debates and disputes over aliens go on and on, and nothing ever changes."

Stuart rubbed his forehead briefly and went on to detail how Central American countries' rural populations were extremely impoverished without access to clean water, sanitation, health care, education, or job opportunities. Rural farming amounted to the sole means of subsistence, but recurring drought rendered much of the land barren.

"It's unfathomable that the gangs in these areas have been in operation for generations. They even include former members of the military, intelligence agencies, and active members of the police.

Unthinkable! But true. Transporting illegal drugs north comprises the bulk of their activity. Organized crime in Guatemala alone is involved in marijuana and poppy cultivation, human trafficking, kidnapping, extortion, money laundering, arms smuggling, adoption rings, and other illegal enterprises. This isn't classified information. We've all previously and incessantly been watching the headlines on the news channels and reading the published articles presented by the New York Times and the Wall Street Journal." Stuart felt compelled to emphasize the unpleasantness of the current situation. "The facts are clear. Thousands of people leave their homes in Central America to embark on a perilous journey, arriving at the U.S. borders daily. Some of the reasons they leave everything behind are straightforward and basic. There are no jobs. Food is scarce. They are afraid for their lives. They are afraid for their children.

"And so, they head north. Few have cars, some take buses or pay others to take them. Many hop trains which is insanely dangerous. Some walk, involving a congregate of other perils. There have been tens of thousands from the poorest, most ravaged areas of South and Central America, coming where they are willing to relocate, to work, and to raise families in safety."

This was the meat of the matter. Henry took a short sip of his iced tea and pushed his chair back. Hands slid toward his pockets. Zigmund Zellovitch mouthed his empty pipe. Will Dalton squirmed in his seat, his large frame growing stiff from sitting for this prolonged period. Stuart resumed speaking.

"Hugh Gallwith, House Representative from the 28th District of Hidalgo county, has invited us here and will be joining us in the morning. We'll visit Brownsville, where the center I mentioned cares for children at a foster refuge, on to Central Processing, and ending our day at the Border Station in McAllen."

"And…our role here in Texas is?" Zigmund questioned.

"To educate ourselves by seeing firsthand what is occurring at our border. To arm ourselves with the knowledge of the day-to-day experience." Stuart's enthusiasm surfaced.

"And do what exactly with this information?" Zigmund had moved forward in his chair and was tamping his empty pipe against his plate.

Stuart squared his broad ex-military shoulders. "I see two outcomes. First. Whatever our jobs are…whoever we encounter in our daily lives…this trip must affect our interactions with others. Immigrants, natives, relatives, friends, and coworkers. We need to spread the word, and by our example, the information that we learn while we are here. I personally believe it will be an enlightening endeavor for each of us.

"I'm counting on all of us to use our professional platforms to share the experience of our visit."

"You're not politicizing us? Winding us up and sending us forth like little tin mice?" Zigmund's sarcasm was taken in stride.

"Absolutely not."

"What's number two?" Zigmund asked.

"I want the congressional reps here to witness the conditions. We all need to recognize how the dramatic increase in the percentage of asylum claims have created a year-long backlog. How a six hundred percent surge has brought America's border security immigration system to the point of collapse.

"I want input from you, trauma experts. There may be some room for attention to the mental health of these people. How can we address the trauma? If I can nail that, maybe I can get some money allocated… All I expect from this group is to agree with and or contribute to a report I will present to the oversight committee at some time in the future. That's it. No more, no less."

"Glad to help," Zigmund responded.

"Yes." Ingrid and Will spoke at the same time.

Henry nodded his agreement.

Stuart allowed himself to smile and taste his tea. Others at the table politely chatted over the tasty sopapillas. The gravity of the situation occupied another seat at the table.

THIRTEEN

Professor Harris-Hunt wrestled a stack of quiz sheets from her tasteful pink leather tote and slapped them to the desk. Regret for her agreement to oversee her colleague's classes agitated her nerve endings. She scribbled her name on the chalk board before facing the students. Sleepy eyes stared back at her from under uncombed hair or baseball caps. It was 7:00 a.m. and most were only partially awake. The others were radiating apathy.

"I'll be filling in for Professor Novak for the next two sessions this week. My name is on the board. My office hours are on this sheet, take one before you leave. Today, there'll be a brief discussion on chapter nineteen regarding analyses of variance and covariance as general linear models followed by a quiz." There was the expected groan from the peanut gallery. It was near the end of the semester and the students needed to be sharp. There was no pity.

"Open your texts and check out the sidebar on page four seventy-two. This is…" the lecture commenced, she barely addressed the students before her, more likely enjoying the sound of her own voice.

Students who had not been fast enough in the registration process ended up in the early classes. Often, they were unhappy about that unfortunate outcome. Professor Harris-Hunt enjoyed the sunrise and a cup of latte on her lavish patio but having both her schedule and some of Henry's, especially this early class, was dogging her time. She was energetic, and she had stamina, but those were virtues she pulled out when they benefitted her. Doing a kindness for someone else was outside of her playground.

The period went smoothly due to few questions from the class. Most listened with at least one ear and others grumbled during the quiz. Still others neglected to pick up her office hour page even though they laid their quiz practically on top of it. She postulated they were college students and no longer needed to be babysat, which she was not about to do. One female from the middle row took a particularly long time walking from her seat to the front. Her curvy body filled out a pair of faded jeans, and her long springy hair fell gently across her caramel-colored skin. Large almond eyes scrutinized the professor's features, manicured nails, gold jewelry, and tote bag. She did not speak but appeared to catalog everything about the female professor before exiting the room.

Priscilla had her necessities gathered and was walking toward the door. The same younger female came before her and breathlessly stated she needed to be sure she signed her quiz. Patience was not a virtue possessed by this professor. She suffered the fools poorly. Students were in line barely above fools and interruptions were unwelcome. Without recourse, Harris-Hunt stopped, opened her leather tote, produced the papers, none of which were nameless.

"I'm so sorry, Professor." The girl claimed. "Having a quiz threw me a little and I wasn't certain if I put my name on it. Glad I did. Thanks." With that she departed once again.

Priscilla sighed with minor restraint. She was due on another floor to teach her own class on Psychological Physiology. She planned a surprise quiz in that class as well. She straightened her slender shoulders and moved briskly down the hall, catching the eye of various male students. A passive smile formed on her glossy lips as a seductive memory eased through her mind.

Despite the shameless pleasure she derived from playing her spider and fly game, she had to admit some of her emotions were edging sideways. The young man was surprising her in a few unexpected areas. The laughter he brought about with his wit now that they were comfortable with each other, his undeniable physical appearance, and the way he took the lead in the lovemaking, all combined to provoke feelings that were common in younger, inexperienced females. Priscilla was beset with these irritating contradictions. She brushed away the idea she was genuinely interested in the jock like brushing aside a wayward strand of hair; but the sensations inside her were persistent.

If she found herself daydreaming about Jamison, reality would surface, and she would have to admit their differences were too great to ignore. It was those times she would tell herself to enjoy what was happening and not look further. She could do that. She could wrap herself up in the moment and had always been satisfied with that much. A little annoyance, like a mosquito, kept buzzing around, and she could not swat it away. This irritation perturbed her. She liked this guy in a way she hadn't planned for. It aggravated and puzzled her. Being vulnerable was not one of her better qualities.

Her days were filled with routine classes, papers, professional meetings, prep for graduation, and a rendezvous here and there, carefully planned and executed. The former predictable and boring; the latter surprising and thrilling. She juggled all with little effort, even maintaining her position as faculty advisor with the student Psy Chi organization. Those duties were minimal. An assembly to attend each month, a slim slice of her time now and again. A tolerated amount of mingling with the students of psychology and their questions.

If truth be known, even the addition of Dr. Novak's classes did not subdue the distinction of spring in the air. Warmer days ever so slightly debuted on the Virginia campus, and with it arrived the renewal of energy and expectations. Priscilla Harris-Hunt was feeling optimistic.

FOURTEEN

Children were temporarily cared for in Brownsville, at one of the locations funded by the Office of Refugee Resettlement. The Catholic Charities organization that staffed the center was under the direction of Sister Mary Benedict who stood outside the front door when the rented minivan carrying the group of visitors drove into the parking lot.

"Good morning!" Sister greeted the group as they exited the vehicle. Her smile was as wide as her voice was cheerful. She had vowed herself to service, but her clothes were no signal. She wore loose-fitting Wranglers, a tucked in Texas Ranger's baseball jersey, and a blue bandana around her neck. Her height was an inch or two above average, strong hands, and a tight gray ponytail that even a Texas breeze wouldn't loosen.

She stepped out to receive the visitors and easily transferred a vibe of acceptance beneath her energetic exterior. She ushered the group into the former Walmart building to escape the heat. The magnitude of the operation was instantly evident. Busy workers who had been extensively vetted were helping children of various ages in a multitude of situations.

The first stop was Sister's personal office. It was a tight space and the six of them would not find enough chairs along with her and a man who was already seated inside.

Hugh Gallwith, the representative from the 28th District in Texas, stood up. He had a generous smile that he shone on each of the visitors. A size forty-six long, light-weight sport coat hung over the back of his chair, leaving him in rolled up sleeves, a loosened tie, and a shiny belt buckle the size of Austin. He vigorously shook the hand of each of Stuart Samson's group and nodded at Sister Mary Benedict. His voice was resonant and metered when he thanked the visitors for coming to Brownsville and to the refugee facility in particular.

"Let's let Sister Mary Benedict show us around her operation," he suggested while he backed the others out the door. Sister assumed the lead and described the facility in proud detail.

"This is where children over the age of seven are cared for while their parents are detained in McAllen. This facility is geared toward the needs of minors. It provides three healthy meals every day, individual beds, educational lessons, learning activities presented in a fun manner. There are Spanish and English language skills. Medical provisions." She spoke over her left shoulder as she walked ahead of the group.

The well-maintained building was clean inside with a nod to the needs of children. Color was splashed as often as possible on walls in the form of paintings and posters, cheerful animals, and happy faces. Furniture and fixtures were designed for short legs and tiny fingers. Even the floor had green and orange arrows giving vibrant directions.

There were several workers along with children, tending to the preparation of lunch by way of stacking trays and folding utensils into paper napkins. Cooks toiled over pots and cutting boards behind the stainless-steel counter. A tempting meaty aroma wafted from the kitchen and encircled the visitors, suggesting a tasty meal would soon be served.

Sister moved through the dining room decked out with colorful polystyrene chairs and low tables. She automatically stopped to pick up a few crumbs from the floor that only she noticed and walk them to the trash barrel near a door leading to a hallway.

In one of the rooms down the hall, three dozen active kids were completing schoolwork in a classroom setting resplendent with bright banners, colorful scenery, alphabets, and recognizable pictures that read in both English and Spanish. *United States of America* stood in tall letters next *to Estados Unidos*, on a banner above the door; both surrounded by stars and stripes in bold red, white, and blue. Shelves stood around the perimeter of the room with crayons, pencils, books, markers, tablets, and uncomplicated texts. Sister moved to a wall and straightened some stacks of worn coloring books and puzzles before placing them on a lower shelf. All the while the children and workers acknowledged her with a wave or a smile but continued as if her presence and actions were as common as chicks in the barnyard.

"The wonderful supplies, these capable, flexible, bilingual workers, are all provided through grants and donations." The nun stopped with evident admiration on her face while the dark-haired heads of the children bent over their worksheets. The small group moved out of the room and farther through the maze toward the innards of the building.

Sarah remarked, "The shower and restrooms are spotless! I wish my house looked this clean." Still, Sister Mary Benedict paused to grab some towels from the dispenser and wipe two hairs out of a sink.

"The children share an amazing work ethic. Boys and girls are willing to pitch in and clean up after themselves. Of course, they have separate facilities…" Her voice trailed off, but the smile widened. "Here are the sleeping areas. Again, gender separate. Each child has their own small cot."

Henry warmed at the sight of a stuffed animal or special blanket on top of some of the bunks. A memory of his grandson back in Virginia brought a sigh with deep appreciation of his blessings. Sister bent above several beds and straightened out coverlets that bore wrinkles only she could see.

The group continued to follow Sister Mary Benedict who talked about the daily routine and schedule. She described the workings and accommodations of her center explaining the ability to create a welcoming atmosphere and attend to the needs of the children while balancing on a precarious budget and abiding by regulations imposed by distant law-making agencies.

"Your program is impressive, Sister." Stuart was standing in the meeting room next to her office where the small group had come to a stop. "Appreciate your time. Looks like you're a busy woman."

"Thank you."

"She's a hands-on leader. Nothin' she would ask someone that she wouldn't do herself. Gets down and dirty. Heh. She dug the vegetable garden out back herself. She plants, weeds, and cans the veggies. Smart, stubborn. . . I wouldn't want to tangle with 'er." Hugh Gallwith chuckled to himself, but his admiration was evident.

"Got any questions?" Hugh offered to the group.

"So, this facility is run by Catholic Charities and funded by the Office of Refugee Resettlement. Did I get that right?" Zigmund was asking.

"Yessir. And don't forget donations!" It was Hugh who fielded the question.

"The rules and regs come from an entirely different department then."

"Right again. Policy comes out of the Department of Health and Human Services." Hugh Gallwith adjusted his tie back up to his neck. He unrolled his sleeves in preparation to don his jacket. He continued in a noticeably different tone.

"The conditions surrounding the crisis at the border are all but un-American. The U.S.

administration needs to focus more on the circumstances in the home countries, Mexico, and Central America, where most migrants come from, my opinion. We need to get to the root of the economic instability and violence so people can be prosperous and safe in their own homelands. We, the United States, should invest in security on the ground and stabilize the economy for the three countries hardest hit by gang violence and poverty; Honduras, Guatemala, El Salvador." The good ole boy drawl had worn off and the politician continued.

"A conversation with Mexico also needs to take place, so they will do more at their southern border to create a safe environment for people migrating into Mexico."

"Sounds like you have spent a lot of time considering the situation." Stuart said what the others probably surmised as well.

"It's my back yard. It concerns me and my neighbors, my constituents…It's just the right thing to do. Honestly!" Hugh Gallwith shook his head just as a boy walked up to the nun.

"*Madre, por favor.*"

"Excuse me," Sister said to the group as she followed the child. They stood as the boy took her hand and led her away toward the cafeteria.

"Any other questions, or anything else you want to see?" Even as Hugh Gallwith spoke the words, jacket on, body facing the hall before the entrance of the building, it was apparent that he was wrapping things up.

Congressman Samson took the hint, glanced at the others gathered in the space, and within a respectable amount of time replied, "I guess we're good. Thank you so much."

"Alrighty," said Gallwith, indicating the way to the parking lot.

"Please relay our gratitude to Sister Mary Benedict," Ingrid Schultz caught Mr. Gallwith's eyes.

"Sure 'nough. I have some things ta take care of, but I'll see y'all this afternoon at the processing center." His twang returned with his wide smile as he headed for his white Chevy Blazer.

Stuart was about to climb in the rental when a green and white border patrol vehicle appeared through the dust that the departing Chevy Blazer kicked up. It came to a stop and two women got out and walked into the building. One wore the uniform of a border agent and the other was shorter and dressed in dark capris, a t-shirt, and new white sneakers.

"I wonder if that's a mom," Ingrid's question was spoken aloud. "And I wonder if she is about to be reunited with her child." Her pitch rose.

The members of the group looked at each other and no one moved any farther to board the minivan. Suspended in a moment of eager anticipation, each waited in mid step. Stuart spoke for all. "Hold tight a minute." He backtracked to the building and disappeared inside. Hopeful excitement built up between the group.

"This could be a wonderful experience to witness," Sarah stated through a budding smile. Others nodded.

Stuart returned after a delay with a pleased surge in his step. He motioned for the rest to come back. One by one they responded to his gesture and followed him inside to an empty classroom.

FIFTEEN

Ingrid stood beside Sarah who was thumbing a response to her daughter via cell phone. Pleased expressions of anticipation crossed the women's faces and seeped through their bodies when they glanced toward each other. Stuart adjusted his glasses. Will's thumbs looped his belt and Zigmund, located several paces farther down against the wall, remained silent. Eagerness charged the air. The clamor from the busy hallway filtered into the room, coupling with expectation as if there was a collective appreciation for what was about to happen. Henry stood quietly at the end of the human chain.

The agent from the truck entered the room first. Ochoa was the name on the patch above her right breast pocket. She was followed by a quivering Latina woman. Agent Ochoa spoke the woman's native language in a calm, voice as they passed the visiting group and made their way to the other end of the room where they waited near a small table with child sized chairs. Stuart and his group might have been wallpaper for as much as the woman even noticed their presence.

The woman's fresh clothing fit her loosely and hung long on her frame. Her thick, dark, hair held a few waves that dropped unfettered just past her shoulders. She continued trembling and wringing her hands as she stood with the agent near the chairs.

Henry's watch first fell upon his fellow professionals who were smiling in anticipation for the spectacle unfolding before them. He stifled his nervous urge to whistle.

Agent Ochoa seated herself at the table with the woman of about twenty-five to thirty years named Verdi, who intensely stared toward the doorway at the end of the room. With unsteady knees, the woman took a step when Sister Mary Benedict walked in with a small child by the hand. The mother gasped at the sight of her little four-year-old son whom she had not seen in days and stretched her aching fingers out as he took a step toward her.

"Francisco." She squatted to his level, waiting for him to fill her opened arms.

The young one hesitated, looked up to the nun who had escorted him in, then at the squatting woman in front of him. Sister smiled, nodded her head, and signaled for the child to move ahead. Still, the child was cemented to the floor. His mother was briefly taken aback by his reluctance but regained her excitement with a sudden move in his direction. Moving on her knees, she scooped him into her arms and repeated his name as she buried her face into his neck and held him close.

In a loud burst of fear the child wailed and thrashed his arms. As tight as his mother held on to him, intending to comfort him and herself, he fought to be released from her embrace. The woman was apparently overjoyed to hold her child and remained oblivious to his anxiety. Time wavered while joyful expectation shifted to palpable unease in the adults present. Ingrid looked to Sarah only to find a pale visage, void of expression, in response.

Verdi straightened to observe Francisco's sweet face, and it may have been the first she realized he was railing against her. The team witnessed her expression twist as her brow curled to a confused frown. She glanced up at the nun who stood nearby. A passive smile offered little comfort.

Again, the woman searched her son's eyes for a clue to his behavior but stayed baffled by his indifference. Her fingers slowly loosened as she released her hold on him. Her body language portrayed her hope that he would accept her and return to her outstretched arms, relaxing in the comfort she so desperately wanted to provide. Instead, he slid his small frame away from her and inched toward the cement block wall. This time it was the woman who sobbed.

In passionate gasps she spoke her child's name. *"Francisco."* Tears stained her face. The pitch of her voice rose with urgency. *"Es mamá. Mijo, ven a mamá."* Volume was not the answer. More tears washed her cheeks and moans escaped through her lips from a wounded place in her heart.

"Ooo." She sobbed and called and crawled along the floor after the child. *"Francisco."*

The boy's small hands were spread out as each finger slid flatly along the cool blocks that made up the west wall. As if by magnetic force, his palms remained against the surface. His head lowered, and his eyes were fixed on his navy tennis shoes. What he saw through his tears was not something anyone could guess. His tiny shoulders scrunched up to his ears, with his belly touching the bricks, while he inched away from the fear that he didn't understand. His steps were short like he was, and he maintained the sideways motion. His compact body hugged the wall as his movement was both slow and intentional.

Sister's stillness revealed that she had familiarity with what was playing out. She stayed where she had stood upon releasing the child to his mother and eventually the boy made his way back to her. He was crying in a softer tone as he stepped close to her leg, then behind it before standing still.

Verdi's volume rose to the ceiling as she called out to the child, begging for his acknowledgement. Her shoulders shook with the vibration of her wretched pleas. On her knees, hands lifted to her temples, she appeared to be dissolving in her grief. Muffled moans continued to escape and the pitiful desperation she projected was discomforting for observers. Heavy tears flowed without abatement, hitting the floor with a thud as if weighted with torment. The suffering woman looked to Sister, and back to Agent Ochoa with anguish across her face.

"Por favor, ayúdame." Please help me, she begged them.

Confused expressions passed among Stuart Samson's group. The sickly smell of tension rose from the floor and spread like an infection through the onlookers. Nausea from Verdi's agony gripped each one. The scene unfolding was contrary to expectation and minds scrambled to correct the mistake that would not be soothed.

"Aaaa." Another painful moan. Her hands returned to the sides of her head and she rocked up and back.

"Aaaa." The sound of a sour note, loud and held, offered by an imposing diva during her aria, could not have produced more unease among the onlookers. Verdi's sorrow seemingly tapped the agent who rose from the chair and came around the table. Gently, she rested her hands on the tormented woman's arm. With the slightest influence she directed the woman to stand and allowed her to rest against her own shoulder. Agent Ochoa remained solid and patient while Verdi continued to release her agony through moans and sobs.

"Mijo." The endearment poured out with hurt dripping on each syllable as her body shook against the agent. Ochoa waited. Sister waited.

Francisco returned to a motionless stance behind the nun, but he did not face her or his mother. Instead, he twisted the hem of his tan shirt. Twisted it until it pinched his little fingers. Next, he took the knotted portion of his shirt and raised it to his mouth. His teeth clenched onto the fabric, and he pulled with his hands at the same time. It was a one-man tug of war. The wailing of the woman a few yards away was muted by a shrill noise inside his head. Briefly, he experienced a tentative calm. He remained there content until he realized that woman was again moving toward him. He waited until she was near his barrier. When she stepped to the right, he instinctively shifted to the left just out of her reach. She wove herself to the left, slowly, hoping to gain his confidence but he eluded her. She hung back, taking a few steps away. The child did not move toward her or away. He stood still and twisted his shirt again.

The distressed woman looked at her son. All the joy of expectation about coming together had been erased. Panic surfaced in her eyes. Her hands raised to her head once more but this time she latched onto wavy strands of her hair and gripped tightly. Her body pointed to the right and she paced a few steps, hesitantly swerving left before pacing again. It was apparent that she was lost and struggling.

"Ayy." The pathetic cry escaped through her lips several times. She moved left then right, shifting her weight, changing direction, and repeating the pattern. Her misery was at an urgent peak. Helplessness emanated from her figure like a dismal throb. Tension would not allow the woman to be still, yet she had no refuge. She was alone in a new country, without friends or family, uncertain of her future, attempting to sever her past, and the one reason that

she endured the struggles and dangers of her recent journey now rejected her. The child remained aloof.

Verdi pressed cautiously forward, only to be rebuffed again and again. With each rebuff she lost stamina. Her palms would raise upward as if invoking her god for intervention, but nothing changed. The dance repeated for the better part of an hour until intervention absolutely needed to come in some form. She approached her son a final time, calling his name, identifying herself, expressing her love. The child gave her his back and scurried away. In despair, her body crumbled to the floor, forming a heap of human desolation. She buried her head. Sobs rose in supplication and uncomfortably ceased until a quiet strain overtook the room. The scene unfolding was off the tracks and minds scrambled to correct the division that wouldn't be righted.

The unsettling silence was more than a shuffle-your-feet discomfort. It was dig-your-fingernails-into-your-thighs-and-try not to scream unbearable. The void of sound was jagged and threatening. It did not calm, it did not energize, it was angular in its menace. The color of this silence was brassy, gaudy, an unsettling chartreuse. You would have to look twice and wonder why anyone would paint anything chartreuse. This piercing silence was utter chartreuse in its foreboding ability to disturb.

Agent Ochoa approached, bent over Verdi, and spoke softly, while the woman rocked herself in a fit of bitter rejection. Francisco accepted the hand of Sister

Mary Benedict who led him away for lunch and a reprieve.

As Verdi and the agent rose, Ingrid stepped forward. "What's happening? Are you giving up? Where is the child going?" Her questions flew like arrows at a moving target.

Agent Ochoa's hand was on Verdi's elbow, leading her toward the door. The woman was barely coherent and in need of assistance.

"The child is going to have his lunch. We'll get some familiar things together and try again in a little while. Don't worry, we won't give up." Her smile was encouraging with a woeful tinge of having gone through this before.

The two women exited the room and the six professionals stood speechless and stunned. Ingrid appeared she might burst; eyes wide, mouth open, as she stared at each of her colleagues in succession. Sarah's face was pale, as if a quart of blood had drained through the heels of her feet. Will's hands found his belt loops while he remained quiet.

Zigmund shifted his weight and muttered to Henry. "Trauma…anxiety… at its most damaging. The child is wrestling with reattachment conflict." Zigmund searched for his pipe. "Both of those individuals will deal with this event for a *long* time. Who knows if they will ever come to terms?"

"Let's back off a bit. I feel like I've just witnessed a personal tragedy and I need to give these people their space." Stuart removed his glasses and wiped his forehead with a hankie. "Henry, you okay?"

"Yes." Henry didn't look at the others in Stuart's group. His eyes remained trained on the floor in front of him where the mother and son had struggled minutes before. His left hand came out of his pocket and scratched his head before meeting his right hand for a succession of finger rubbing.

"Anybody hungry. Let's grab a water or a bite at a fast-food place." Will suggested. "Change the scenery."

"Good idea." Zigmund endorsed the suggestion.

Henry stepped out and aside with eyes still lowered. He appeared lost in another dimension with his neurons firing on familiar concepts in his brain. Each of the team members were drifting in their own orbits as they sauntered beyond the room and back to the minivan. Zigmund was the last to reach the vehicle and he leaned toward his collaborator. "Coming, Henry?"

"Mmm."

* * *

"Look, here she comes! Shh."

Six observers stood in anticipation as Agent Ochoa and Verdi stepped onto the playground where Francisco was being pushed on a swing by Sister Mary Benedict. The mother stood in silence, smiling, while she held a fuzzy bear in both hands. Sarah could tell it was not a favorite toy, probably new, because the whites were still white, and the blue was still shiny. It hadn't been dragged in the dirt, spilled on, or loved so much that the fur wore off. The toy was a long shot.

Francisco looked away when he saw his mother and allowed the swing to lose its momentum. Sister spoke to him as she crouched to his level. She took his hand and led him to a makeshift sand box where a few plastic toys lay, brittle and faded by the sun. She scooped some sand into a bucket and handed him the shovel. He mimicked her movements. Without words, Verdi and the agent approached from the side and slowly sat at the edge. Verdi dipped her hand into the sand and brought up grains that she allowed to slip lazily through her fingers. She repeated it a few times and Sister Mary Benedict did the same. When Francisco dipped into the sand, it fell quickly from his little hand. When he tried again, Sister giggled with encouragement. Francisco tried raising his arm higher to release the sun-bleached grains and it blew against his shirt. Assuring him that it was fine, even funny, the sister did the same to herself.

The four continued to dip hands, shovels, and a bucket, into the non-threatening substance, exchanging implements, and fostering trust while speaking in soft tones. The proximity of their bodies became closer and interactions were deliberate.

"Para ti, Francisco." For you, said Agent Ochoa, offering a spoon for scooping. *"Para ti, mamá"* and she gave one to Verdi also.

"¿A mi?" Ochoa asked the boy and extended an open hand for his shovel, waiting patiently for him to comply.

"Mamá," he said and handed the shovel to his mother instead.

Verdi held her breath as she reached her hand out for the shovel, trying hard to mask her reaction. She took the toy and scooped a little sand inching closer to where her boy sat. She flipped over a mound, offered the shovel back to him, and he took it and turned over sand as she had.

"Bueno, Francisco," she praised him, inching closer. He dug, dumped, dug, and slapped the sand, and gave the shovel to his mother.

"Tu turno," he told her in his four-year-old voice. She took her turn with the shovel as the agent slipped away and Sister Mary Benedict backed off to sit on a nearby bench. The mother and child continued to play in the sand before he asked her to push him on the swing.

Henry and Zigmund observed the give and take with measured familiarity. Will and Ingrid slowly backed up while awkwardly silent. They moved toward the lot where the minivan was parked but Sarah took a seat on the bench next to Sister Mary Benedict. She noted the child's body language, the inch forward/pull back approach of his reintroduction. She watched the mother struggle to contain her eagerness to touch her child. It was an emotional dance they *had* to perform to solidify the readjustment. It was difficult to watch. Sarah realized she had little idea what that mother must be feeling. In the end, it would be a definite reunification. They would live happily ever after; but with pain, trauma, untold suffering, maybe nightmares, probably anxiety, and who knew whatever else. Sarah wondered if it was all worth it. Was anything worth all that?

* * *

"Yes, with time they exchanged toys; eventually he asked her to swing him. It was a lengthy process." Sarah filled in the rest of the group.

"What did the sister tell you?" Zigmund fingered his pipe.

"She was quiet. I was thinking that she had mentioned earlier that the children come here at ages seven and above. I wanted to ask her about it, but I felt awkward. If it was a mistake that the child was here, ya know, too young, I didn't want to point it out. Not with all of the other amazing things that she has going on here."

"So, did they leave together?" Ingrid inquired.

"They did, and the border agent went also."

Stuart moved toward Henry as the group approached the minivan. Hanging back just a beat

Stuart asked in a serious pitch, "What do you make of it, Henry?"

Henry spoke with pensive reserve. "This sometimes occurs after an unplanned separation that's not explained to the child. Something he's not prepared for. When the child has no familiar adult to rely on, the length of separation plays a critical part in trusting again, even his own mother."

"Will he be okay?" The hope in Stuart's voice was thick like honey.

"It's hard to say." Henry stopped walking and directed himself toward Stuart. "But I do know this; early life experiences can affect some physiological processes in the brain – for example, neurochemical imbalances related to depression. It could be permanent, similar to neurological impairments resulting from other trauma."

The two men stood still for a moment, submerged in the gravity of what was spoken and what they witnessed. Henry couldn't imagine what Stuart was feeling, he could only remember his first encounter with a client having such a strong personal anguish. That first experience always revisited even after dozens more had occurred. "The brain in early stages of development, such as in this young boy, can sustain damage that has long lasting effects, both mental and physical. Resolution could be a long and difficult process."

Observations and impressions bounced back and forth between the six group members as they chatted in the seats of the minivan.

"I wonder if this is common," Will Dalton said. "It was uncomfortable for me to watch that poor woman."

"Did you notice the border agent? She knew what to do. They both did." Zigmund observed.

Discussion between the group of individuals with years of diverse expertise and insight was respectfully interactive. Congenial comments flew, covering respect for Sister Mary Benedict and her responsibility, and encompassing what lay ahead for them that afternoon, with a few comments about giant belt buckles.

SIXTEEN

The rambling city of McAllen awoke to life with common daily activity. It had the familiar earmarks of prosperity such as fast-food chains, well-known retail stores, mega-groceries, car dealerships, traffic jams, and school sports on Friday nights. The bustling southern city boasted a population of more than 140,000 of which Hispanic or Latinos comprised almost eighty-five percent. The cost of living was low, temperatures were high, rendering the climate and the soil hard and dry in some places. The City of Palms, as it was known, boasting its tall trees along beautiful Main Street, had abandoned its agricultural roots for international trade, retail, and tourism. With the first inland foreign-trade zone in the U.S. as its location, the McAllen Miller International Airport was built to facilitate air cargo traffic.

The North American Free Trade Agreement (NAFTA), ratified in 1994, paired with the Free Trade Zone (FTZ), allowed for cost-saving opportunities for manufacturers, luring businesses, and warehouse services to the expanding community. Wealth followed success.

The growth of the developing city had gleaned its most recent attention due to being the location of the border processing station. Unfortunately, not always a favorable slant. It is noted that, in Hollywood, any publicity is good, even if it's bad. It didn't work like that with other cities. The negative press, both photos and articles, was shining a light on the city struggling under the weight of immigrants dying to taste the freedom of the United States. Literally. Dying.

The current rate of immigrants coming to the Texas border alone, not factoring in Arizona and California as the two other states with border centers, had been compared by reporters to a level five hurricane. Forty percent of border patrol officers were being pulled away from regular duty to attend to injuries suffered by individuals attempting hazardous means to enter the U.S. Officers were pulled away to incarcerate and process swells of individuals dangerously crossing under the darkness of night.

Cartels were alleged as being involved with the influx in numbers. They were blamed for trafficking and criminal activity. History attested to their crafty schemes, proving them savvy enough to send their biggest groups of smugglers across when the migrating crowd was large, and order was displaced by chaos. Criminals had indeed been caught at the border, but the percentage was one. One percent.

The department of Customs and Border Protection (CBP) was in the business of enforcing laws that protect the United States. An officer at the border was there to secure that border, prevent drug smuggling, enforce immigration laws, protect agriculture, and ensure trade compliance. They inspected cargo, people, and luggage to detect illegal contraband, invasive animals, and plants. They worked exclusively at ports of entry under the primary mission of preventing terrorism.

A border patrol agent had a different function and a separate job; usually responsible for larger areas, such as off-road regions with few or no other security measures. Their methods were in a more conventional law enforcement role. Their jurisdiction extended to roughly one hundred miles inland from the border.

U.S. Immigration and Customs Enforcement (ICE), an agency under the U.S. Department of Homeland Security, was not in the business of tricking people, separating families, or lying in wait for aliens who wanted to enter the country legally. ICE was sanctioned to enforce regulations. There were legitimate reasons for restricting individuals who approached U.S. borders without due process. The directives currently in place assisted those wishing to cross the border legally seeking an asylum claim. Those who attempted to enter illegally were detained and faced consequences. Those were facts. However, ICE in its fundamental construct did not necessarily endorse separation of families.

The 2018, United States' Zero-Tolerance policy made entry to the U.S. more difficult under its new guidelines and added to the back-up of procedures already in place to facilitate a legal entrance. The abundance of people attempting to reach refuge were rising in even higher numbers and the infrastructure was faltering. There wasn't enough time, there wasn't enough space, to accommodate the seekers. The administration in Washington planned zero-tolerance to be a deterrent but the immigrants didn't hear about it until they arrived. The separation of families confused and compounded problems for immigrants and subsequently for border stations and agents.

* * *

The delegation had entered the dusty minivan for the second time near noon and readied themselves for the hour-long trip to the border station. They travelled roads paralleling some of the twists and turns of the Rio Grande which was a twelve-hundred-mile natural border between the U.S. and Mexico. Colorado was the source of the swift river which was responsible for some of Texas' lush farmland. The McAllen, Texas central processing center with its palm trees and wooden fencing grew into full view.

Two bulky warehouses were converted in 2014 to accommodate the growing surge of immigrants who came to the border town. The two options that were legal processes of entry included having a previously approved application with a sponsor and completed paperwork or the avenue to asylum. Either of the two methods involved waiting between verification steps and the previous facility was bulging with the back-up of process.

Twenty perspiring people were scattered on or near the steamy sidewalk on the north side of Ursala avenue across from the facility when the minivan pulled into the lot. Some hoisted signs on tall pieces of wood. Some held posters with stark bold lettering. Others chanted 'No more cages. Humans have rights.' It was an unexpected scene in a day that was providing one after another.

With large blue letters on the side and a radar disc on the top, a KRGV Channel 5 News vehicle parked at the curb. A man with a heavy camera on his shoulder stood near a woman with a microphone. All eyes ogled the assorted professionals as they stepped from the mini-van into the ninety-two-degree day that was south Texas in spring. Squinting against the eastern sky, the group assessed the spectacle before them.

The vocal twenty stared at the newly arrived six. The stunned six stood silently across from the peaceful demonstrators. The practiced news reporter and photographer maneuvered to capture the perfect shot. Stuart's team moved slowly until a shout from the minor exhibition reached them.

"Are you here to do something?"

"We're just observing," Stuart Samson replied.

"Well, that's pathetic."

"Yea. It's not a zoo. They're not animals. They're human beings!"

"You're right. There needs to be some changes." Stuart directed his group toward the entrance to avoid confrontation. They distanced themselves from the protestors out of confusion and lack of ability to disagree. Henry swallowed hard at the consideration his small group of cohorts and their modest little endeavor may have twisted into somewhat of a news story themselves.

Fine sand mingling with streaks of sun, impaired vision and generally aggravated those newly arrived. Not to worry, the vista was unchanged for miles, so that what they saw where they stood was the same as what could be seen miles down the road. Trees and cacti dotted the thoroughfare or enhanced the buildings here at the border. The variety of names; living rock cactus, nipple beehive cactus, nickels' cactus, eagle claws, horse crippler, reminded humans to be wary as the plants stood erect and threatening. Tumbleweeds were swept along by a too-warm ribbon of air.

For all the enormity of the station, the sound was subdued with only an eerie undertone whisked about by a steady draft. The movement was constant, with border agents in uniforms and equipment belts, heavy with patrol gear, walking with purpose between the structures and amid the people. Their left shoulders sported an eagle and flag on the navy-blue border patrol patch. The words "U.S. Customs and Border Protection" spanned the top of the insignia and stars accentuated "FIELD OPERATIONS" at the bottom. A gold badge sparkled from the front left chest area. Some wore protective vests outside their shirts while others chose to wear them underneath the uniform. Handguns were holstered. White and green vehicles moved about with quiet motors blending into the beige-ness of the scenery.

It was to this panorama that Stuart's group found themselves privy as they stood on the burning asphalt waiting for Hugh Gallwith to drive up in his Chevy Blazer. The sun had crept over the roof tops of the Texas buildings, but the temperatures were way ahead of the clock. A merciful breeze swept by at intervals only to brush dust up from the roadway and aggravate the adults standing near the heat radiated by the vehicle they had exited.

Ingrid took a few steps toward the sprawling processing building and shielded her eyes back toward the others. She rubbed sunscreen over her nose. Not having been in the sun since the last Wisconsin summer, the threat of burn was real. Will walked in the opposite direction and back again. Henry looked out toward the demonstrators through the wooden slats of a fence around the parking lot.

A cell phone rang, and several hands dove to pockets for retrieval. Stuart came up the winner and pressed an icon on his phone. He stood still while he listened to the voice at the other end, but Will and Ingrid walked back to be near, as if they needed to hear through Stuart's other ear. He ended the brief conversation with a subdued 'thank you.'

"Who was it?" Sarah Applewise asked, checking for messages on her own phone.

"It was Hugh Gallwith. Apparently, his wife had surgery three days ago and Doctors discharged her today. He wanted to take her home and be with her. He apologized for the delay and the change of plans. Said he was going to call someone to meet us."

"What does that mean? Is our tour off?" Sarah's voice was tinted with agitation as she stuffed her phone into her purse. "Did he give any idea how we'll be contacted?"

"He said someone would meet us."

"It's so hot out here." Ingrid offered the obvious.

"It is. I can't take the heat." Sarah fanned herself with both hands.

Henry's hand slid over his hair, but he remained silent. Zigmund side stepped away from the group's body heat. A clammy silence fell over them as they stood in the unshaded lot that sided the building. Each time the door opened all heads swung in that direction with hope raising their eyebrows. A reciprocal glance back at them from the individual who walked off left them disappointed. Several false alarms caused them to lose the raised eyebrow and eventually glance half-heartedly. That was when a man in the CBP navy blue uniform approached them and introduced himself.

"I'm sector chief, Sergeant Cayne," he said, verifying the patch above his right chest pocket. His hand was outstretched.

"Stuart Samson." Stuart stepped forward and shook the man's hand as did Will, Zigmund, and

Henry. Introductions went around the group with smiles and nods.

"Mr. Gallwith contacted me about your visit. He's sorry he couldn't make it, sends his regrets. Let's go inside. Please come this way." Sergeant Cayne opened the door allowing the women to lead to the interior.

The air was cooler inside. The building was bright and businesslike with a police station type ambiance; official, protective, housing employees with special skills.

"Mr. Gallwith previously explained to me about your trip here, so I was expecting you." Sergeant Cayne led the small group through the entrance and into a side office area, but no one sat. "Let me begin by answering any questions."

The shape of his body resembled a fire hydrant, and he imbued the feeling of capability and security. He filled out his uniform with muscle and meat in equal amounts. His head was shaved, and his face held a seriousness that served him. If you were shipwrecked on a deserted island or lost in the jungle, you wanted Basil Cayne there with you. He fielded questions as they came quickly, turning to address each person who spoke.

"Yes, ma'am. We are stepping up efforts to meet the influx of immigrants. Besides the air-conditioned tents erected on property next to the edge of *this* city, which hold five-hundred immigrants each, there's a twenty-five-million-dollar tent project in

Brownsville, which was not intended to house aliens but to provide courtrooms. Expectations are to process up to two-hundred-fifty people a day in each of twenty makeshift courts on federal property managed by Homeland Security…

"No, sir. The policy was never intended to separate families. It was always intended to reunite the children after adults were screened for criminal activity…

"TSA, like all Department of Homeland Security components, is strengthening DHS efforts to address the humanitarian and security crisis at the southwest border. TSA volunteers support this effort while minimizing operational impact…

"Ma'am, TSA stands for Transportation Security Administration. It has committed one-hundred-seventy-five law enforcement officials and four-hundred people from Security Ops…

"No, sir, it *adds* to congestion on some level. Border agents are unpacking diapers, mixing formula, and handing out juice rather than their assigned duties…

"Duties of arresting criminals at the border, arresting gang members, patrolling the borders, and rescuing migrants coming across who are in physical or medical danger…

"No, sir. It was not designed as a jail. It's a processing center intended to hold three-hundred-eighty but currently houses twelve-hundred people…

"Let me just explain one misconception." Sergeant Cayne took a long breath and relaxed his stance the slightest bit, but it didn't show. "If a family wants to come to the U.S. and intends to become citizens, they need to start filling out paperwork in their home country. There are agencies set up to help. There are lawyers who specialize in immigration law. Each applicant needs a sponsor here. It could be a relative or an employer. It's a long process that has certain requirements and milestones to complete. That's way different from someone who comes to seek asylum. A lot of times asylum seekers are scared and running for their lives. They show up with the shirt on their backs, no papers, and no idea of what it takes. They just want to come in."

"What does it take to be granted asylum?" Zigmund needed clarification.

"The people either come to the station and surrender or they sneak in and when we find them, they surrender. They're not aggressive, they comply. They go to the processing center, get an initial interview, and basically tell their story. The information must be reviewed, verified, and passed on to a court hearing. Each of those steps takes time. It takes years to process the hundreds of thousands of cases with so many waiting. The back-up is huge, which is why people don't stay at the border. The immigrants come in, have an initial interview, blend into a community before their second hearing, get a work permit, put down roots …"

"Where do they wait?" Zigmund again.

"That's just it. We ask that they stay locally to be available for the second hearing but if they know someone in the U.S. many just go. We use ankle monitors, but they complain about them too. There are so many more coming now. There are migrant centers set up in lots of cities for the ones waiting. There are missions and soup kitchens. Some of the immigrants go back to Mexico to wait. There are little tent cities near the border where they stay."

More questions flew. Sergeant Cayne responded. "The unaccompanied minors are referred to the Office of Refugee Resettlement, ma'am.

"Yes, ma'am. Unfortunately, we have uncovered that traffickers sometimes send a child in with an unrelated adult because they know that if they cross the border with a child, they are only held for twenty days…

"It is correct that some traffickers 'recycle' the children and use them over and over to get adults into the U.S…

"No, sir. I am not personally aware that twenty-two or twenty-three-year-olds are posing as children. I have not experienced that first-hand…

"Ma'am, the first screening interview is to determine a credible fear of persecution if the individual returns to his home…

"Yes, sir. It is true that several U.S. states welcome and depend on migrant workers for cheap labor…

"Sir, you are correct. The U.S. has no plans to vaccinate migrants currently…

"I can tell you from personal experience that child deaths are rare events…

"Yes, ma'am, and I'm happy you are here…

After nearly forty minutes, when all inquiries, pertinent or insignificant, were satisfied, Sergeant Basil Cayne assigned an interpreter to simplify communication as the group commenced with the tour.

Dr. Zellovitch thumped his empty pipe in the palm of his hand while his scrutinous gaze skimmed the walls. Sarah Applewise had some information that caused her to be enthralled with her cell phone to the exclusion of her companions. Her expression belied irritation. Stuart was on an actual call and had stepped off to the nearby hallway for privacy among the throng of people.

Henry contemplated the enormous amount of information Sergeant Cayne had provided in his ever-efficient manner. He sorted the different agencies in his brain, attempting to identify and keep them straight. Border Patrol, ICE, Customs and Border Protection, Office of Refugee Resettlement, DHS, TSA. The facts were staggering. It was a scenario he was learning about like a Marine, on the job training. Combining Sister Mary Benedict's operation, Hugh Gallwith's opinions, and Sergeant Cayne's statistics, the specifics were coming at him like a flock of geese, and he felt like he needed to duck.

SEVENTEEN

Henry had felt tired for weeks before the trip commenced, and he brought his state of fatigue with him to Texas. Even the excitement of finally arriving at the processing center had not engulfed him. Some of the others may have been anticipating a personal contact but he was not. He moved among the group as if being pushed by a strong wave. The experience of the reunification debacle unsettled him and rendered him acutely conscious of where he focused his eyes. He heard the protester's words in his head, reminding him these were not animals to be viewed. A tingle ran across his shoulders in response to the discomfort.

Now brushing past the slow observation team, a young man with a border agent patch on his sleeve was leading a string of nine bedraggled individuals. Each carried a fresh bottle of water, some held it to the backs of their necks, while others drank as they moved. Henry counted four children out of the group. The body heat in the corridor spiked the temperature as the tired and dusty people shuffled through. The scuff of ragged shoes was the only sound the little band made.

Henry observed the rhythm of their gait. He noticed the dirty windblown hair in need of shampoo, the tattered t-shirts, and ragged pants. Some of the children had parched lips cracked by arid days in the sun. One of the adult men had dried blood where a jagged cut on his leg had happened and partially healed. All had tired eyes. Henry looked at their backs as they passed him as if measuring. *How far had they come? How did they get here? Why did they leave their home? Who stayed behind?*

A female agent ushered the aliens through a metal detector and a steel door into an area already crowded with others. The group squeezed in between the many that were huddled in an open section with a half wall of plexiglass. None were handcuffed. None were belligerent. They were waiting. All were waiting.

The upbeat young agent spoke Spanish to the seekers. She offered them coffee and juice. She told them where the restrooms were. She answered questions. Will stepped forward and asked, "These people did not come through the terminal. Who are they?"

Border agent Angie Santiago answered him in English. "They were found this mornin' on the road this side of the Rio Grande Valley. Border security was makin' their rounds and found 'em wanderin'. Brought 'em in."

"Does that happen often?"

"Ever' day. Sev'rl times ever' day." Angie was holding an empty tea can from a vending machine and she spit into the opening.

Henry's eyes stayed fixed on the rag-tag band of immigrants sitting on benches against a wall, squatting, laying on the floor in the confined space of the room. Questions stacked up in his mind. Still, he couldn't move past the contradictions. The building was clean, well lit, equipped, and functional. There were engraved emblems on the wall in honor of The U.S. Customs and Border Protection Agency and one of the Rio Grande Sector. The workers were dressed in blue uniforms, complete with embroidered patches, and equipped with firearms and protective gear. The seekers were worn-out, frayed, but hopeful. Henry wondered if this was where hope came to die.

"Might we speak to them?" Ingrid was asking an interpreter. Her name was Liza Booker and she recently came from South Carolina with an M.A. in linguistics. Spanish was one of the six languages she spoke.

Liza looked over to Angie Santiago who was standing close enough to hear the request and nodded.

"Rather than overwhelm them with all of us standing in, why don't you speak, and we'll stay back. Ask where they are from. How they got here. Where do they plan to go?" Ingrid suggested.

Liza, young, slender, and fresh-faced, stepped over legs and shoes before squatting in front of a couple huddled together. The delegation heard her well enough but only a few of the words were familiar to Henry. Fortunately, one woman spoke back, seeming to give a long explanation. Liza faced others in the group, repeating her questions. A thin gentleman sat up and spoke in his native language. Another man next to him bobbed his head in agreement. More voices rose until active chatter was coming from each end of the sizable room. The tired and weary were telling their distressing stories to the pretty young woman who spoke like them.

Henry's hands slipped into the genial pockets of his loose-fitting trousers while he stood rapt in the human scene unfolding before him. The spirit in the room was buoyed through tales of each person, explaining their journey and their pain. He couldn't wait to hear the interpretation, although the body language had already conveyed much.

Liza remained squatting like a baseball catcher for what seemed like 'ever' until everyone had spoken, explained, and was satisfied she had heard them. Her hand raised in the direction of Stuart's band standing engrossed on the sidelines. The immigrants nodded and smiled and a few clapped. A form of *'gracias'* was heard from some. A lean gentleman with gnarled fingers rose and came around the corner to shake hands with Henry, Stuart, and Will. His face was weather beaten with furrows as deep as hoed rows of earth and he moved back with slow steps to the spot he had left, resuming his post to sit and wait.

Liza straightened and came to face the consortium. As if heavy with information, she sighed before speaking. "There is a lot to tell. We could go to the station lunch-room, and I could relay what they said."

"Will they get lunch?" Henry inquired about the seekers.

Overhearing this, Angie Santiago affirmed they would all be fed. There were nutrient bars available along with packs of cheese and crackers. Not exactly lunch, but food, nonetheless.

"I guess I could use a drink. Water, that is. Okay, let's go." Ingrid took the lead this time. Henry was satisfied to remain passive while mulling events in his mind.

Back at the modest lunchroom, the congressman's group sat on plastic chairs. Will leaned his elbows on the oval table. Liza Booker, the young interpreter, reviewed the statements made to her by the asylum seekers. Youth was tempered by her professionalism. Animated, with deep green eyes and straight hair, she explained the similar stories. This group of immigrants had traveled together for the Mexico stretch of their journey which originated in Guatemala for five of them and in Honduras for the rest.

"Three of the aliens from Guatemala were one family: a child and her parents. They left about five weeks ago, on foot. They lived outside the city of Petapa and old gang members were brazenly kidnapping children to recruit. If there was resistance, they beat the children to intentionally show their force. This family was afraid for their child. Basically, for themselves all together."

"My god," Ingrid whispered, "…and they walked all the way?"

"There were others from the area too that told much the same. The gangs were long established and vicious. Another family said their village was poor and dry. Nothing would grow. They told me they had no food, no jobs. There was no reason to stay."

"Before we left, I did some research." Will spoke up. "Central America's income is among the most unequal in the world. The wealthiest ten percent of the population owns nearly half of the national wealth, the poorest ten percent owns just about nothin'. This makes for a struggling middle class. Land or money is concentrated in the hands of the few, making it tough for poor workers to improve their situation." Will sounded like a news reporter with his facts and figures, but all the info was sound. Ingrid wanted to know what else the seekers said.

"A few in the room were Hondurans. The poverty sent them north too. There just wasn't work for them, not consistent work anyhow. They paid what they had, all of what they had, to get a ride part way and walked the rest. Most didn't know what to expect when they got here but, I guess they all believed it would be better than where they came from."

"Why did the man shake our hands?" Will drank from a bottle of water and listened attentively to all that Liza had to say.

She blushed and lowered her head before she spoke. "I told them you were smart people who were observing the situation to go back to the government and suggest how to help."

Ingrid closed her blue eyes. Henry imagined she was bracing against the weight of such an expectation. The burden of responsibility hung in the air, heavy and grave. Henry flinched with the onus of such an idea.

Will looked from the young interpreter to his colleagues. Ingrid was now making notes on her iPad. Her strokes were quick. Henry was structuring an equation consisting of human elements. If he looked like his brainwaves were far away it was because that was true. Stuart spoke up.

"I think Hugh has an actual agenda for us. Right, Sergeant Cayne?"

"Yes, sir. We are going to. . ."

"Henry, are you coming?" Ingrid asked the man to her left. "Henry?"

"Mmm? Yes, fine." He raised himself from the chair and followed behind the others, unaware of where they were headed.

EIGHTEEN

In 2014, Border Patrol Central Processing moved to a converted warehouse in McAllen. The 'situation' was known as the "child migrant crisis" due to the overflow of families and children taken into custody after crossing the U.S. border. The building came to be called "Ursula" because of the street it was on.

Interpreter, Liza Booker, walked ahead of the rest and spoke to Agent Angie Santiago. Henry caught snippets as they chatted between sidesteps and interruptions. Occasionally, the agent would spit into her aluminum can without missing a step.

Liza had recently come from a few days working in Clint, Texas. Judging by the few things he gathered from her remarks about it, the place was experiencing overcrowding even worse than McAllen, if that were imaginable. He kept his eyes lowered and took slow steps as he stayed within earshot.

"I guess a judge ordered that somethin' had ta' be done. Anyway, a bunch a lawyers came through and kicked up a hornet's nest. After I interpreted for them for two days things got intense. I was moved here after that."

It was the matter-of-fact way that the words spilled out of her mouth between bites of a granola bar that grated Henry's nerves. *To what extent had the repetition of tragedy desensitized the workers? What had they seen? Was anyone addressing* ***their*** *mental health?*

Before he could dwell on those questions his attention was drawn to two men walking the corridor from the opposite direction. Each of them held a single paper that seemed heavy in their hand. With slumped shoulders the men filed singly past Henry and on down the corridor. Something made him question the interpreter and agent.

"What was that paper?"

A revealing pause allowed Henry to imagine the worst and hope for the best.

"Probably their tear sheets," agent Santiago answered passively.

"May I ask what that is?"

"While a parent is separated from a child, they have to go through the processing to see if they'll be prosecuted or not. The paper tells them that's been completed, and they are going to leave the facility."

"Now they get reunited with their child?" Henry's voice was recognizably buoyant.

The agent measured her words while her feet kept moving. Her voice was slow but clear.

"It can go either way." Santiago spit into the can.

"Meaning what?" Henry slowed his pace.

"Meaning he could be deported. OR, he could be detained, and his child could be taken to a foster facility. The tear sheet explains how to find the child later and what the next steps are." Agent Santiago was not without feeling, however, at this point they had reached the end of the hallway which opened to the fifty-five thousand square foot holding center. A sight in its own regard. She stepped forward.

Henry drifted into the immense room with cathedral-like ceilings, shiny channels of silver duct work, and what appeared to be miles of chain link. The space sprawled out before him like some human rodeo arena. Tall cage-like enclosures were separated into four immense sections and comprised the center of the expansive hall. It was impossible to see all the divisions from where he stood. A perimeter of green cement passed around the enclosures and served as the walkway margin. The enclosures had swollen beyond capacity. It was not any wonder why the migrants called it *"la perrera,"* Spanish for the dog kennel.

No words came to Henry while his eyes widened to take in the enormity of the scene. Dozens of dozens after dozens of faces met his gaze while he stood planted in the boundary that lapped around the interlaced stretch of fencing. He stared at the scope of the situation despite himself. The men inside the holding pens moved freely yet the movement was minimal. The people closest to him and his group looked out at them with a combination of curiosity and resignation.

Henry saw every height and build a man could display wearing t-shirts in as many colors or logos as he imagined ever manufactured. Behind the men and their t-shirts were many more faces that he could not view from where he stood. With some were their children.

The high ceiling of the converted warehouse still portrayed the essence of space from the lofty rafters at the same time the ground level was beyond crowded with frayed humanity. The bright lights stayed on day and night and the effect withheld a certainty of time and date which lost its relevance long before. Each person had a green mattress inside the fencing, but the space was so cramped the narrow pads touched each other at all sides.

The air inside the big room was cooler than the entrance area. Almost chilly. The mixture of sweat and overused portable toilets combined with some anxious human pheromones and came across like tangible pus in the air. Such an odor met a person at the door and clung to their nostrils with ferocity. Some of the agents wore face masks in a nod to the unpleasant condition. Henry dug in his back pocket for a hanky. He rubbed his nose in defense of the smell.

Sergeant Basil Cayne was speaking to Stuart Samson only ten feet away but the conversation was muffled by the undertone of scattered chatter among the agents and detained. Henry was certain he heard a voice in clear English pierce through the crowded figures to exclaim, "I'm not a criminal." It was repeated.

The simple words touched Henry's raw emotions like a razor blade. He heard it and he listened to what had to lie beneath. He did not know if anyone else had heard the man speak out. The words were steeped in a mixture of desperation and frustration.

Henry imagined himself exchanged for the man's position; fenced in, uncertain. The discomfort lingered past the instant that short term memory encodes or drops a message. *I'm not a criminal.* Indeed.

Voices in unanimous expression rose and circled the individuals in the spacious building. Air conditioners roared to alleviate the oppressive heat from outside and were equaled by the undertone within. From time to time, an agent wielding a bullhorn blared a brief message barely audible above the crowd.

Henry was aware that his group was moving on, so he pushed himself to fall in. A tall wooden stand much like that for a lifeguard or tennis judge, was positioned at the demarcation point where the male area ended. An agent sat at the top overlooking the crowded conditions. After the men section came the second, third, and fourth sections; boys age ten and up, girls age ten and up, women head of households with their small children. These were being monitored by walking agents, agents sitting atop the wooden stands, and mounted cameras.

Sergeant Cayne described sanitation stations that contained a dozen portable toilets and sinks that were cleaned twice a day. There were showers and a laundry facility.

"Migrants are offered wet wipes, crackers, chips, juice and other snacks while they wait. We distribute mylar blankets because when the mattress pads run out the migrants sleep on the concrete floor.

Young migrants and unaccompanied children are offered sweatpants, t-shirts, shoes." He waved his arm across a sizeable bin with plastic bags of unused shoes and clothing waiting to be distributed.

As Henry came to the end of the men's enclosure, avoided the latrine station, and advanced toward the children area, he was shaken by the reality that the pictures he had seen on the news had not adequately portrayed the level of gloom. Here the sight was overwhelming, and the faces of the people were real. The sheer number of confined humans was beyond credence and many were children.

A steady flow of adults in uniforms were walking along the aisles. Inside one fenced space, a social worker was holding a child in her arms whispering and rocking back and forth on a cot. Henry watched her eventually rise and carry the child to a rocking chair positioned in the enclosure where they both eased into a steady rhythm. It was a sweet sight to the old man who had been overcome with a plethora of emotion in a short stretch of time. Henry remained stationary as he perused the children in the vast space.

A few yards ahead a young one cried. Henry strained to see where the low-pitched sound came from. He spotted a long-haired child, small in stature, standing at the chain link with fingers entwined in the mesh. This child's cry was steady. Henry headed in that direction. On closer inspection, he was able to determine the child had a runny nose, dirty face, and the denim shorts were wet. He made his way to the outside of the fencing and squatted. He spoke to the child in English as he would to someone that might understand him.

"Hey, little one. You are so sad. What makes you cry." The child did not desist, nor did he acknowledge the amiable voice of the old man.

"Tell me what's wrong. I can see you're upset."

The child continued to cry, toddled away, and stood alone. He walked farther and stopped in the center of his enclosure where he grew a bit louder. The woman who had been walking in the aisle came up to Henry.

"Julio's next." She held a diaper, wipes, and powder. Her look moved swiftly from Henry's face to the keypad on the gate. "Sometimes they regress to wetting after they get here even if they're older." She moved in a fluid motion inside the enclosure and picked up the unhappy child. Henry could hear her calm him in his language. She held him briefly before lying him on the mattress to relieve him of wet clothes. The wet denim shorts were kept to be washed. Young Julio was left in a diaper and stained shirt, but the tears that left his dirty face streaked, had halted.

Henry lingered outside this fence after the woman finished and moved on. Back at his level, Henry offered more words in soft encouraging tones. Julio looked from atop his mattress. Dark round orbs of endless depth peered out. Henry sensed a pensive acceptance. He tried to imitate the few words he had picked up while in Texas.

"Hola, niño. I'm Henry. Hola." He pointed to his chest and repeated his own name.

The child studied the man behind the chain link. A short thumb found its way to his mouth and a subdued comfort relaxed his body. Henry repeated the two Spanish words. Julio lay his head down, thumb in his mouth, his little legs came up and curled around his bottom, eyes never straying from Henry's face. In a moment's time, droopy lids covered his tired eyes and the thumb slipped out of place. Henry was immobile. One of his aged hands laced the metal chain-link as his head bowed examining the floor. He sensed the weight of gazing eyes.

On the mat next to Julio, an older boy was standing, watching Henry. This child was taller than Julio, wearing torn clothing, in need of a bath and a haircut. He studied Henry with an intense regard.

"Hola." Henry tried again as he shifted his regard toward this child. "Hola, niño."

Henry squirmed under the scrutiny of penetrating eyes and realized an isolated sense that there were only the two of them in the space. "My name is Henry. Hola." The calm tone of his voice was genuine. Henry smiled with his lips and remained motionless. Unabashedly, the boy looked over the man who squatted on his haunches; who knew what he might be thinking. Henry tried once more.

"Hola."

"Hola." It came in a faint whisper without any other movement. It was a single word, but so much

more. The boy persisted to stare at Henry from his side of the chain link enclosure. Henry rose to move slowly closer to where he stood. Aware that any simple movement might be misinterpreted, he was deliberate and measured. The boy's eyes did not waver.

"Hola, niño."

"Hola, senor."

"My name is Henry. Henry." He articulated his name and pointed to himself. He pointed to the child and raised his eyebrows in expectation. Nothing.

"Henry," he said again with a hand to himself then a hand toward the child.

"Mateo."

"Hola, Mateo."

"Hola, Enri."

"It's nice to meet you, Mateo." Henry spoke the words and smiled. The boy had not moved more than his lips. He did not seem invested in establishing friendship. Questions swirled around inside Henry's skull. If he had an interpreter there were dozens of queries to ask. The one assigned was speaking with Stuart and someone in the men's section. He would not interrupt.

"How old are you, Mateo?"

The boy maintained the observation of him.

"How long have you been here?"

Nothing.

Henry internally berated himself for limited communication skills. While still feeling inept he heard steps that grew louder and closer. He pivoted to face a uniformed border agent with his name on a patch. Sergeant Ortega.

"Hello, sir. Can I help you here?" The question was congenial.

"Oh, Sergeant Ortega, I was just trying to converse with the child. I'm afraid my Spanish is poor."

"Can I help?"

"I hate to bother you, Sergeant. Do you know anything about this boy, his family, his circumstances, how he got here?"

"He's been here a little while."

"What is he waiting for?" Henry's question was earnest.

The agent walked toward one of the station desks and picked up an iPad. Henry stayed back near Mateo and tried to speak again.

"Adios, Mateo."

The boy looked up at Henry. His body had not moved, nothing had changed. Henry felt as if there was an alteration in the brief connection and he moved away toward Sergeant Ortega with a nagging feeling he had failed at something.

Sergeant Ortega ran his finger side to side on the iPad. A row of numbers corresponded with numbers on the enclosures. His finger moved up to verify something before swiping across.

"I think this young man came in a week ago. His mother is in an adult tent."

"A week. Is that common?" Henry focused on the upside-down name illuminated in the iPad. Mateo Elmar.

"Not really…but I don't know the whole story."

"Does the file hold any other information?"

"I'm sorry, sir. I cannot give out information. What I can say is any family seeking asylum will have to prove that going back to their home will be dangerous and/or life-threatening." The sergeant swiped and the screen darkened.

Henry shifted from one foot to another upon hearing the unsettling facts. He glanced at the child in the cage, at the blank screen, and lowered his head, while futile hands slipped into the pockets of his trousers. He thanked the man and walked toward the exit of the tent where the others of his group were standing and talking.

NINETEEN

Later that day, Henry found himself standing just east of McAllen outside a forty thousand square foot tent encampment that had taken thirteen days to build. Contradicting reflections pawed heavily through his mind encompassing what he had seen and heard earlier. The congressman's group still led by Sergeant Cayne was being directed around one end of the camp. The temperature encouraged beads of sweat to form on Henry's forehead and under his shirt. *Must be a hundred and five.* Will Dalton's shirt was a shade darker with perspiration after only a few minutes outside.

Henry marveled at the solid construction. The air-conditioned tent was sturdy, well-built of extremely thick, durable fabric, and securely fastened to the metal poles mounted around the sides. A mixture of stone and pea gravel surrounded the base of the dense synthetic material in the sprawling field that had been repurposed. The muted exterior color was reminiscent of military, or at least some serious function; no comparison to a circus were conjured from the appearance of this tent. No doubt about the expense of this project. It took a lot to build and maintain the resolute facility.

Inside waited thirty-six shower stalls, forty-eight-inch flat screen TVs, DVD players and children movies, five hundred beds, and new clothing. There were medical supplies prepared for arrivals who may be sick or injured. This spanking new structure was not yet at its limit, but numbers continued to climb.

Henry was walking with his group toward hundreds of people milling inside. Many uniformed agents were attending to duties and assisting immigrants at tables or in groups. One woman was breaking pieces off a cracker and feeding her toddler. Small knots of women and children sat on benches or lay on mats. Henry watched a child snuggle into its mother's arms where they both eased into a steady rhythm. The sight encouraged a smile to cross his face.

A child's cry rose from a far side of the compound. The distant pressing sound soared above the drone of the electrical units and human voices and spanned the tops of the rafters. Henry stiffened. Simultaneously being caught off guard as well as recognizing the unmistakable element of fear in the voice, Henry's deliberations dispersed. He realized the cry was an indeterminable distance from where he stood, but his head moved to face the sound. He strained to see where the high-pitched wail came from but too many bodies blocked his view. While this child continued to bawl, a second resonance echoed from a new far-off location. When minutes had passed with Henry immobilized, no less than four children's voices could be detected in a chorus of pleading strains; each emanating from a different area yet engaging and supporting each other. Though the voices were young, the pitch was piercing, and their disharmony was distinct. It was as unpleasant a sound as one might ever expect to hear. One that would linger long after quiet ensued. A disharmony, if you will, of frightened innocence.

Unfazed, Sergeant Cayne zigzagged between the seekers and tried to keep the group informed about what they were seeing. To stem his own discomfort, Henry smiled and nodded to the people he passed. The echo of the crying chorus was still ringing in his ears when the group came upon another distressed tot. Sarah spoke to the little one as Henry bent to do the same. The child continued to cry, toddled away, and stood alone. He walked farther and grew louder. A small brown woman who had been a few yards away came up to the child.

Her scrutiny moved swiftly to Henry's face and to Sarah. She moved in a fluid motion to pick up the unhappy child. Henry could hear her calm him in his language. She held him briefly before sitting him on the concrete to wipe him with a wet sheet she pulled from a plastic envelope. She had no comb for his hair, but she used her fingers to push the strands from his face. She smiled into his eyes and gave him a gentle squeeze.

By now the sun had touched the center of the Texan sky and begun it's slip toward west. It did not mean the temperature was dipping. Inside the cool relief, Henry accompanied Will, Ingrid, Stuart, and the interpreter, in out and around the groups of women with children.

Stuart engaged some of the ladies with a bit of their language while he kept moving along. Ingrid shook hands with a few seated women. Sarah and Zigmund had moved ahead of the rest and were out of sight.

Henry asked permission to speak to some of the women as he passed. The interpreter explained his kind words and his smile told the rest. A few of the detainees were willing to talk. Henry imagined the rest were trying to remain calm and were not interested in prattle. It amazed him that anyone was eager to answer a question or offer information, but he also realized that it was probably occurring repeatedly.

"Where is she from," one of the group would ask and Liza Booker would translate.

"Tegucigalpa."

"Acapulco."

"San Miguel."

The list went on. The stories went on. No work. Unsafe. Searching for a better chance. Henry would listen intently to similar pieces of a human jigsaw puzzle that affected so many lives. There were a few words that came up repeatedly and the small band of outsiders were becoming acquainted with the familiar sounds of *"coyote, bandito, agotado, temerosa."* None of them pleasant words.

"Could you ask if any of them is Mrs. Elmar?" Henry was thinking of the child back inside the McAllen enclosure.

Liza Booker stepped between the ladies. She wove her way in and out of aisles and bodies where there were no aisles. She spoke the name before calling it out louder. She made her way back to Henry and shook her head.

All six of Stuart's group had regathered with Sergeant Cayne near the center of the tent. Few of the detainees looked up toward these visitors now. The energy and curiosity had been sucked out of them. Liza tilted her face to Henry in an expression of *do you want me to keep asking*?

Henry met the question with his lips squeezed tight. He had no right to ask anything of anyone.

"Elmar," Liza yelled. *"¿Senora Elmar?"* She stepped a few paces farther. "Elmar?" One woman out of a group met the gaze of the agent from a distance.

"Please, ask where she's from," Will suggested.

The dark-eyed woman answered only what she was asked. Liza Booker repeated it in English.

"San Jose Calderas, Guatemala."

"Explain who we are. Ask why she came here," Will prompted.

The woman's gaze fell away, and a pall overtook her features. She drew a long breath from somewhere deep within where perhaps a small reserve of strength resided. Liza Booker softly translated as the words fell from Rosa Elmar's lips.

"We lived outside of San Jose my whole life. We had a little garden and I sold eggs from my chickens. We hardly had enough to eat. Five years ago, we heard about Aprode. It was a project to help the community of San Jose Calderas. Senor Lopez came, he trained men to be guides up the Acatenango volcano so tourists would come and spend money. My husband, Eduardo, got a job as a guide two years ago."

The group of six visitors had collected closely now to listen to the translation; their eyes fixed on Rosa. They stood as a combined statue as she unfolded her story.

"The job was only part time but for once we had some money. Our boys had shoes, so they went to school. We had enough. But…"

The team hung on. The small woman pulled her hair back with thin fingers, then rested them on her lap. Another heavy breath followed. Liza continued to translate.

"After this blessing came the evil. It followed the money, wanted a piece. Bad men followed the workers, like my husband. They approached him and some of the other guides. They wanted a percent, but our money was so small. They did not care. They threatened. Said they would hurt them so they could not work. The police said they had to catch the bandits in the act, with a gun, with our money. We figured they were not going to help us. At first the guides tried to just hold out."

Rosa's voice trailed off and her weary shoulders sagged. The thin fingers grasped her bony legs through her worn clothing. Liza Booker lowered her eyes.

"At first, Eduardo wouldn't tell me. Later I found out the bandits came every Monday, following the guides to their home. Harassing them. Making threats. He even paid them some money, hoping they would leave him alone."

The woman's anguish came through each word. Henry silently waited, glancing sideways at the others. His stomach tensed with a vile feeling about where the story was heading. Liza continued to translate.

"Eduardo went to work one day and one of the guides reported in late. His family had been threatened by the gang members. They cut his wife and his little boy. We were all so scared after that. Eduardo hoped he would be spared because he had given money. The bandits said they were part of Barrio 18, but Eduardo said they were just punks, wanna-bes, just trying to scare us with the name of the big gang. They kept demanding more. Kept following him home and the others. We did not know if he should go to work anymore. But they already saw where we lived, all of us families.

"We were afraid to leave our homes. Whenever Eduardo was at work I worried, I would not let my boys go outside. Not to school. We talked about maybe leave San Jose. We knew other people who went north, it was possible. We talked about when the season was over, we might have some money to move.

"After the guide's family was hurt, no one said anything about it; like they were afraid to let tourists know the danger. Everyone had come to rely on the tourists who wanted to go up the volcano. The bandits did not come around so much when the hurricanes blew; the work season was over. We just survived like before. The next year, when the tourists came back, so did the bandits. Eduardo said he would pay them something, but he also bought a gun. It made us feel safe, but…we were foolish.

"Halfway through the good season, lots of tourists, lots of money in our small community, the bandits came one night. Eduardo was gone for an overnight trip up the volcano. They must have known. I heard the small engines on the motor bikes. I heard them yelling, waking up the town. Bottles smashed on the bricks. The young men laughed and pissed in the street. Our house was tiny. I told the boys to get under the bed. I prayed for God to spare them. I heard the heavy steps and banging on the front door. I did not answer, I was afraid to move. My boys were crying under the bed and I told them to hush.

"The door caved in and a drunken punk walked into my house with a bottle of tequila in one hand and a knife in the other. He told me to get up and come to him. He was just a teenager, but alcohol made him brave. I got up, thinking I could lead him away from the bed and my sons. He tipped the bottle to his mouth and walked to me. He put his wet lips on my forehead, his stinky breath in my face. He wanted money. There was a jar hidden in the fridge where we kept it and I gave him all of it; six thousand, five-hundred pesos. He laughed at me; wanted more. I told him that was all we had.

"He threw his bottle on the floor and it shattered. He grabbed my hair, put the knife to my throat. I closed my eyes and said nothing. I felt death coming. He shoved me aside and walked toward the bed. I held my breath, but he walked right over to my boys and told them to come out. I screamed 'no, don't do this.' He did not pay any attention to me. He stamped his dirty boot on my floor right in front of the bed and demanded the boys come out. When they didn't obey, he reached his hand under and dragged my oldest from the floor. I could see him crying. He looked at me and I was quivering, covering my mouth with my hands. He was so small, so young.

"The bad man shook him back and forth like a puppet. I yelled again and grabbed the bandit, tried to make him let go. He swiped the knife at me, it cut through my shirt and blood ran down my arm. I pulled his hand away from my son, but it made him angry. He pushed me down, stomped on my chest, grinding my back into the broken glass and spilled tequila. I was stunned for a minute. When I could move again, the bandit had dragged Pablo out the door and I ran out, telling my youngest to stay under the bed.

"The other bandits had gathered right in front of my house. They were on the motorbikes. They pushed my boy around, back, and forth, until he stumbled. When I came close, they grabbed me and kicked me to my knees. One dragged Pablo up by his hair and forced him on the back of a motorbike then rode away." The woman's breath was irregular and forced. Henry expected her to stop; almost wanted her to.

"I ran after. I screamed. Neighbors came out and stood on the sidewalk, watching. I ran but could not catch them. I ran after them even when they had rounded a corner and I could not see them anymore. I kept running. I kept running."

Rosa hung her head in her hands, and the sound of her weeping lifted through her fingers. Each of the individuals listening felt distress just hearing her pain. Liza Booker seated herself and put an arm around her shoulders. She whispered something in Spanish that sounded soothing to the by-standers. All waited.

"We found my son two days later." Her voice rose to a pleading pitch. "They had carved an X on his chest; his throat was slit." Words squeaked out of her mouth from a broken core deep inside "He was in a hole with mud and maggots…" Raw sobs wracked her hunched body; distress enveloped anyone within earshot. "He was nine years old. Nine!"

Liza told Rosa she did not have to continue. She told her that these people were here to help, but that her sorrow was too great. Rosa went on.

"The people in our little town were frightened. They didn't want any more harm in their lives. It wasn't safe for us anymore, so we made a real plan. When we figured the time was right, we took what we could carry and left in the night. We rode on buses for days; out of San Jose Calderas, out of Guatemala all the way to Mexico City. The buses were hot, and they smelled like vomit. We were tired, hungry, and so afraid.

"With each day, we felt safer, farther from the bad men. We got to Mexico City and hoped we could stay there for a time. We had to work so Eduardo took a job here and there, building, hauling, selling; whatever work he could find. I stayed with our youngest son. When there was no work for Eduardo, I worked; cleaning, cooking, washing. That lasted several months. We saved what we could.

"Eduardo came to me and said that he met someone who could get us to the border. He would take all three of us and we had enough money. I asked questions. Who is this man? How will he take us? Will we be safe? Can we be sure? There were no answers. I had lost my son; I would not risk the other. But Eduardo said this man could be trusted. He told me he would meet with him again in a few days, if it did not feel right, he wouldn't do it. After the second meeting, he said we should go. There would be a truck of people. We would be safe; the man would handle the guards along the way. It would be taken care of. We could make it to the U.S.

"I was not confident. Who was this man? How could he guarantee our safety? Why would he help us? But I was more afraid of what might find us if we stayed in one place. If Eduardo said it was good, then I trusted him. We had to do something."

By now the woman's story had overwhelmed Henry and the others. They were engulfed in the words Liza relayed. Ashamed to stare at her in her grief but too drawn in to turn away, Henry's eyes and ears were trained on Rosa.

"The man took all of our money for the passage. The truck was worse than the buses. It was jammed with people, no windows, no air. The first day we rode inside the whole time. It was hot and people were sweating, thirsty, packed close together. It was impossible to know if it was night or day. Nobody talked because we were in darkness. We just kept moving, bumping, and bouncing against the sides and into each other. There was not enough room for everyone to sit; some had to stand.

"Late at night the truck stopped once and we got out for a short time into the blackness. Everyone had to pee or shit. There was no privacy. No toilet papers. The next day there was a stand with tortillas that a woman gave us for free. The bottles of water were warm, but no one complained. There were trees for peeing in private. The driver said we could stretch for a few minutes but had to keep moving. We rode the whole night and into the next day. We were so tired, but it was hard to sleep. The air inside was thin, and the smell…

"The truck stopped once for us to get out and two other times. We heard men's angry voices, arguing. Dogs barked outside the back of the truck, but the doors did not open. My son was so scared, he buried his face in my shirt, I buried my face in Eduardo's. It took so long before the truck roared up again. The next day the truck stopped for the last time. The driver came around and opened the back. The sun was low but still stunned us all with brightness after the dark inside. It was hard to move after staying still for so long. We got out. My boy was wobbling. He was sick.

"We all looked around us and there was nothing. No town or city, no trees, or hills. No train track not even a real road. There was a sort of gravel path. The driver told us to follow it. Said this was as far as he went. Said there would be a town several miles ahead. He gave us each an apple and bottle of water. 'What do we do in the town? How do we get to the border?' We looked at each other. The driver told us get to the town and a man would get us to the tunnel. He hopped back into the truck and headed in the direction he came from. No one spoke. There were seventeen of us. Some set out along the gravel path. Eventually, we all followed.

"We started walking late in the day, which was a little cooler. We were tired, and hungry, but more afraid to stop than anything. We had to watch low for snakes. We looked up for helicopters but there was not any place for us to hide if we saw them. The three of us fell far behind because our boy was struggling to keep up. Sometimes, Eduardo would carry him on his back. We tried to keep the others in sight; by now they were far ahead."

Rosa Elmar stood up and her lungs released pure anguish into the air. She looked at the Americans, the border agent, all the women around her, and back to Liza Booker. She spoke in a tone that sounded more tired and weary than before.

"We made it to the little town. We got food from a soup kitchen. The missionaries had an old building there because of all the seekers. They let us stay and rest. We were there two days when a kid came and said he would guide us to the tunnel. The padre trusted him and said we could too. Said the kid had gone before.

"The kid wanted money to take just the three of us. Said small numbers were best. We gave him two thousand pesos. It was all that was left.

"It was an early morning, and we were almost there when four men stopped us." Her words were laced in disgust. "They were ugly and filthy. I could tell it was trouble. They demanded money to pass. The coyote did not know them. Even though he had a gun there were four; he ran. They pushed my little boy to the ground. They beat Eduardo. Punched him over and over. Kicked him when he fell…"

Liza's face was tilted up towards Rosa who was standing over her. Rosa's cheeks were drying where the tears had made tracks; dark hair swayed as her head shook from side to side. She had done well. She had made it to the border with her son. She had told the story as far as she could. Now, the enormity of her situation appeared to have cemented over her and weighed her down with misery.

Ingrid mumbled an apology and moved to leave the woman to her anguish; but stopped again, transfixed. Henry lowered his head and relegated his hands to their pockets. Nauseous with the images just described, he remained immobile near the frail woman in the tent. Several minutes passed.

Liza translated hesitant words.

"The men came at me…" Rosa's eyes peered off into a distance as if watching a catastrophe play out. She appeared to shrink inside the clothes on her body and her hands trembled with their personal memories.

"Ahhh." The sigh she breathed had its own agonized voice. "Edwardo was hurt very badly… there was so much blood. He could not make the last few miles. He said we had come so far and sacrificed so much, he insisted we go the final distance. He said he would be okay if we were safe. I didn't want to leave him…" Gasps and tears combined to interrupt the story… "but I couldn't help him…"

She took a dozen breaths; the burden of her situation rising and falling with her chest. Her hands pinched and squeezed each other while her words came back with an evident effort.

Liza Booker told the others. "In the end, she took her son and made it through the tunnel to the other side. When border patrol found them, she was taken to the adult area and her son was taken where the children stayed. She hasn't seen her husband at all and her son only two times," the translator relayed the last part.

Rosa looked directly at Henry and pleaded with him to reunite her with her child.

"Por favor, por favor, senor. Mi jiho. Por favor, ayúdame."

"Si, señora." It was the little of what he could say in her language even though he did not recognize her plea for help. He acknowledged with a nod. The struggle that she conveyed was wrenching to hear; her emotions made just standing there feel insensitive but leaving her held a cruelty that did not set right. He could only help by listening, hearing her painful account. She was crying, begging. It was a mother missing her child, worried and afraid.

The interpreter translated the words he spoke. He validated her fear, not by saying that he understood, because he could not. Reassuring words chosen carefully expressed his acknowledgement of her pain. There was no denying her love for her son and he believed all that she said. These reassurances were accepted by her. The woman rocked back and forth where she sat; her dark eyes drying and looking off in the distance.

Henry debated about saying that he had met her boy. *Would it upset her or reassure her? If he was only seven, why wasn't he here with her? What had the agency explained to her?* His confused eyes probed Sergeant Cayne's face. The man who he wanted with him in the jungle was not the man to whom he would point out mistakes. He kept his silence.

An unpleasant listlessness floated up from the surrounding area. The seekers were free to move about inside their enclosed space and some walked up and back with their babies Some stayed immobile. Mostly, they blended into the colorless atmosphere.

Fade kept coming to Henry's mind. These people were *fading*. They were losing strength of will, losing focus, losing the hope that got them so far. Hope was fading on this spot as he stood a fence away from Rosa Elmar and absorbed the damage she expressed.

TWENTY

Shame engulfed Henry back in his hotel room for the simple reason he was glad to be there. He was relieved to be alone and away from all the painful distress he had witnessed. He berated himself for not speaking a language that might have allowed him to offer a bit of solace to the wounded souls he had met. An expectation surfaced that the other members of Stuart's group would want to discuss their experiences of the day and the idea drained him.

The day had presented one heart-wrenching event after another. The spectacles of desperation and the sounds of misery reverberated through Henry's bones and his stamina was depleted. If he could just rest for a bit before dinner his mood may improve. The hotel bed was just waiting to oblige him.

First the shoes came off his tired, hot feet. The trousers slid down and were laid over a chair. His already rumpled and sweaty shirt found a sufficient spot in a heap on the floor. Henry slipped between the sheets and immediately the stress dropped off his body. Relaxation was a welcomed gift. His worries drifted up slowly until they hit the ceiling and burst open and away like so many bubbles. He slept.

The room phone buzzed. Another buzz. Henry reached a wrinkled hand to pick up the receiver. It felt like three minutes had elapsed while he had been asleep, but it was an hour and twenty. Stuart was on the other end. "Henry? Will you be joining us for dinner?"

"I'm sorry. I drifted off. What time is it?" He wrestled the sheets to sit up.

"It's seven."

"I'll be right down. I'm deeply sorry to have kept you waiting." He hung up the phone with a jolt and jumped to his feet. They were supposed to gather in the lobby at 6:30. *I should have left a wake-up call.* He didn't expect to be able to sleep so easily, or so soundly.

"I apologize for my tardiness," he explained when he finally joined the others. They all looked somewhat tired themselves, clothing a bit puckered, similar to their faces. "I dozed off."

"We've decided to go for Italian. Sound okay?" Sarah asked him while fishing for a buzzing phone in her purse.

"Sure, whatever you like."

"Back to the rental." Sarah jerked her head up and alerted everyone.

Over salads, pasta, meatballs, and sausage, the group babbled about random subjects.

"Extra preparation for the Boston Marathon coming up in two weeks. Ever been to Boston, Henry?" Zigmund Zellovitch was reading the ticker tape on a TV screen near the bar.

"Yes. Crazy traffic. Not my favorite place to drive." Henry's listening consisted of waves of attention alternating with distracted preoccupation as the others spoke about the day's observations. The discussion was animated and questioning from the start, with conjecture regarding levels of anti-social behavior, separation anxiety, trauma manifestation, fear.

"Well, today was a new learning experience for the six of us, I'm presuming. It is for me. We've absorbed a lot of information and learned a few novel words in Spanish." Ingrid forced a smile, her voice elicited affirmation from the polite group.

"Having the interpreter proved to be an important link, obviously. The people were willing to talk about themselves to her. They were tired, some a little worse for wear. I made a mental note 'hopeful'." Will gave his impression of their early encounter. "One similar element was that where they had come from offered nothing to stay for."

"Yes," agreed Ingrid. Henry absently nodded.

Sarah observed, "Several of the children ignored the others nearest to them. Is it a type of isolated self-preservation? An attempt to stay in control of your own space, albeit small and austere?"

Zigmund agreed with the minimal interaction among the smallest of the children. "I'd call it panic and interrupted attachment," he offered. "I have worked with many individuals who have withstood trauma. I usually meet them long after the event, of course. Even though it's painful to discuss what happened to them and difficult for me to hear, by the way, today, ahh, particularly poignant."

Will was jumping in the discussion and simultaneously taking time to Google several facts that he wanted to verify. He eagerly shared with the team.

"This Barrio 18 that snaked its way through Guatemala…is a ruthless web of gangs. They are into all manner of criminal activity. Name it and they've done it. Interesting about the Acatenango Volcano. It's become a profitable tourist attraction after the long-time civil war in Guatemala."

"People want to go there to climb the volcano?" Ingrid nibbled on a breadstick.

"For sure. They travel there to have the chance for a one-day or two-day guided trip up the volcano. I guess it's amazing."

"I appreciate your efforts to keep us informed. The personal visits had made the deepest impressions on me." Ingrid spoke with her modus operandi of obviousness, but the others nodded their agreement. "I sensed the tension among detainees. Their uncertainty was palpable." Ingrid sipped her drink and consulted her cell phone notebook.

"Some of the children *did* talk to us," she pointed out. "In fact, one little boy told us his life story." She smiled as she spoke, possibly thinking of the child and his missing front tooth.

"Yes, Ingrid, but think about this. It may be the story he was told to tell by someone who had coached him." It was Zigmund, pipe in hand, reminding them all about the unseen forces at play. It was a valid point for them to consider.

"Where would one expect a child from Honduras, who had trekked over a thousand miles to reach Texas, begin his description? It was unfathomable to think about what awful things he might have encountered before *and* after he left his home. If that little boy were, in fact, one who was repeatedly used to accompany an adult across the border, he surely would have been told what to say," Zigmund said.

"I remember him stating he missed his mom, he was happy to be in the United States, and his dad had all of their papers. I guess it does sound a little trite. Henry, didn't you get a little boy to talk to you?" Ingrid sipped long and glanced toward him.

"We exchanged a few words." He kept his eyes lowered, replaying the modest chat.

"Some of the adults were actually expressive; pleading may be more appropriate." Zigmund resettled in his chair. "Their frustration was evident in their chosen words and their dispirited body language. My observation included individuals with depression--non-communicative, withdrawn. There were others with anxiety--pacing, crying. It was a noticeable contrast to those we saw who had just been 'rescued' and were still hopeful."

"Of all the places we've covered, the processing center which I found both enormous and overwhelming…" Will's eyes focused on the tabletop. "We visited with the adult ladies in their tent. We toured the child foster center. I have to say, everyone has been wonderfully accommodating."

"Excuse me." It was Sarah. "What did they say was the average length of the waiting period again?"

"It varies." Stuart had remained silent and listening, but now fielded the question. "First of all, if they've gone through appropriate channels, maybe secured the help of an immigration lawyer, have a Visa and application papers, and have a sponsor lined up, they aren't even supposed to come to the border station. They go through the process at the consulate in their home city or town.

"If someone sneaks over the wall or tunnels under and are caught, they stay until their background is investigated for previous attempts, and for prior criminal activity. Agent Santiago explained it to me. They must prove they were in danger at their home and would be in peril if returned to their origin. You can appreciate how intricate and tedious *that* investigation can be. They go before a judge, must wait for the investigative process, then a second hearing. It can take a*n exceptionally long* time. Then there are those who are returned within a week."

"Who are they? What is their circumstance?" Ingrid's eyebrows raised as she questioned.

"Probably no sponsor, no papers, no established threat back home. Agent Santiago said some of the immigrants hear they can cross the border, and there is work just waiting for them. These lies come from the coyotes. They take all of the money a family can pay and promise them a wonderful life." Without him saying more, his words made a deep impression on the team.

"Some detainees stayed on their mattresses most of the time," Sarah stated her observation. "I did see some men pacing along the fence walls."

"The faces of the children struck me. They were so…I don't know. Blank. Detached. Almost like they didn't know what to do." Ingrid strained for the words she needed. "I guess they wouldn't know what to do. Everything was so strange to them. I still can't imagine what these people have gone through."

"The male section was definitely the most crowded. Pressure of the unnatural situation was present and with it there was observable aberrant behavior. Except," Zigmund lifted his empty pipe to his lips. He seemed to chew on it and an idea simultaneously. "Except for the men with children. Did you notice?" He looked to Henry. "The men with children held them, sat with them on their laps. They did what any father would do in any other large group situation. Kept them close. Protected them. Instinctual."

Before Henry could comment, Sarah spoke again. "An agent explained to me that little communication took place possibly due to continuous turn over. He also said no uprising or discontent existed among immigrants inside. The facility ran smoothly overall, according to him."

"Why was it so cold in there?" Ingrid asked and shivered for emphasis. No one replied, nor disagreed. "And the odor…"

The waiter came around to relieve the guests of a few of their plates. "Would anyone like anything else?"

"Can I get another glass of wine?" Ingrid raised her empty glass.

"I'll have another iced tea. Anyone else want something?" Stuart glanced around.

"Wine." Sarah smiled and leaned back against the metal chair. Her face portrayed a jigsaw puzzle of notions.

"Another beer for me," Will said as he drained the glass to hand to the waiter.

"Henry? Zigmund?" Stuart prompted.

"No, thanks. I'm finished," Zigmund said.

"Water for me, please." Henry looked at his plate with a few abandoned swirls of pasta lounging in sauce. When his mind was over stimulated it did not make sense to eat, he was reduced to concentrate in one area. The plight of the people he had met that day kept coming back to take center stage and spaghetti was relegated to the wings.

Will spoke again. "Did you see the row of tables set up with the folks at computers? I first expected they may have been contacting their families but found out they were having interviews on-line."

"You mean their intake interviews?" It was Zigmund.

"Yea, I'm pretty sure. They answered several questions about their intentions. The process takes hours in person but most of the interviewers speak Spanish which is a *huge* asset. Still, it's difficult to get the information straight but they do a great job.

"My impression of the seekers was also hopeful as you mentioned. I did not personally witness any fighting or unruly behavior. Most were attentive and cooperative while some were dealing with apparent depravation or handicap."

Zigmund spoke next. "The immigrants have already waited for a long time—weeks, months. When they finally get that interview, I believe some think they're 'in.' They are asked to remain local, but they sort of blend in, maybe in McAllen or maybe farther north. The process becomes even more difficult after that. Do I have my facts correct?" Dr. Zellovitch looked around. His words were a sticky mixture of syllables, thick with inquiry. One could almost hear the gears inside his brain.

"I can't believe our agencies have to interview and investigate everyone that comes. It's an unimaginable amount of work! No wonder there is such a back log. No wonder there is so much waiting. And the stress…no wonder." Ingrid expressed her discomfort with the process. "Henry how does the stress really affect these people. What is the level we're dealing with here?"

Henry pushed his unfinished plate of food toward the center of the table. He rubbed his lined face with one gnarled hand while gathering his words and remained silent for a full revolution of the earth, while the burning stares of his associates melted his eyelids. At last, he ran his hands across his rumpled trousers and met the eyes of Ingrid Schultz who was farthest away from where he sat. Expectant ears strained to hear what he was about to say. He was overcome by a weariness that zapped much of his grit.

"Toxic stress for a child is a prolonged exposure to serious adversity without buffering protection. Protection like having a parent close by, stable family relationships, and pleasant familiar surroundings. We are hard-wired to react to stress by fight or flee. The process is chemical. When we can't run or fight, the adrenaline and cortisol build up. Long term activation of the stress response and overexposure to stress hormones can disrupt almost all a body's processes. It can harm a child's developing brain by interrupting the normal maturation process while introducing hardship. The result is short- and long-term health problems. Physical and mental health problems. Long term stress has adverse effects on adults as well.

"The worst scenario is for the children who have been separated, even though the facility we visited this morning was designed around a child's needs. Anxiety at an early age comes without the benefit of ability to reduce that anxiety; a child develops coping strategies that work but ultimately are unhealthy. In other words, what might help a frightened child get through a day may be a devastating development in the long term.

"I believe this current situation has caused damage beyond our ability to measure. Your best efforts," he looked at Sarah and Stuart, "will bring about recognition of a grave situation and my hope is that there will be adequate and appropriate adjustment to the policies sometime soon. I agree that today we witnessed a traumatic event, but there was much more happening in that room." Henry sighed a hundred-pound sigh before he continued.

"A child who was separated from his mother and, after time, relates to his caregivers is nothing new. I admit this was a short span of time, what five, ten days? You all know the Stockholm syndrome?" Familiar with long standing psychological research involving prisoners who eventually side with their captors, a few nodded their heads.

"This is similar. We could record our observations and confidently affix a diagnosis." Henry paused to collect himself. "Given the criteria that were met; emotional symptoms with distress, social impairment, the only lacking qualifier was duration. But the problems that small child was facing were just the current issues. Who can say what might develop in the future? And don't ignore the impact these *workers* are absorbing daily. I keep coming back to this facet of the setting that intertwines with the reality of the immigration condition. At what point will the agents' kindness, patience, ethics, run out?" He was certain that at least Zigmund, his colleague, was familiar with the Zimbardo experiment of August 1971, involving college students tapped to play guards or prisoners. After only six days, the 'guards' took on punishing characteristics and the experiment had to be halted. His deliberation continued.

"At what point will one immigrant look like every other and become more of a number, or worse, an irritation, rather than an individual human being? Pain, suffering, and trauma have visited upon all these people. Not just the ones seeking asylum. We have to be mindful of this area of the dilemma." He nodded to the agreement of his peers and leaned back against his chair.

Zigmund concurred with a slight nod of his head and long draw on his pipe.

"It will take time for the reintroduction of family members, even the closest, to feel safe and secure." Zigmund extended the explanation. "What we observed today is simply the tip of the iceberg that is the entire immigration episode for a family. How are we to comprehend the trials they faced in their homes and neighborhoods? What sent them on a mission to seek refuge so far away? Something tragic led them here but they probably didn't anticipate this division of family!" An awkward discomfort settled as Will, Sarah, and Ingrid reached for their drinks.

"Was it just me, or did anyone else get the sense that the little boy who didn't want to go to his mother…this in not irregular?" Ingrid asked.

"I got the same take-away." Will offered his unpleasant insight with furrowed eyebrows. "Apparently, both Sister Mary Benedict and the agent had seen and handled this situation before. Can't say I could have done anything differently if I were in their place. But, how discouraging that it's, you know, common."

Henry surmised that Stuart's thoughts were already in the process of making some sort of proposal once he was back in Washington. He would be the most appropriate to instigate change of all of them seated at the table, along with Sarah's endorsement. *Go for it, Stuart.*

"I'm so sorry." Stuart reached in his pants pocket. "I usually turn my phone off, but I guess I forgot. Please excuse me."

"Go ahead, take the call," Will said.

"Yes, by all means," agreed Zigmund.

"It's Hugh Gallwith," Stuart explained when he looked at the I.D. "Hello." He rose to step away.

"Tomorrow we'll be heading home. Plane leaves at one something. Probably need to head for the airport around 11:00 so we aren't late." Sarah took Stuart's absence as an opportunity to inform the rest. "Makes sense to me that we plan to speak about our experience here. Anybody got ideas how to use this trip to educate and inform?"

"Well, I—" Will was cut off by Stuart's return.

"Again, I apologize for my phone. Hugh wanted to tell us all once more that he regrets not being here this afternoon. Wants to make up by treating us to a nice breakfast in the morning. Someplace called 'Sweet Temptations.' Said he would meet us all there about 9:00 a.m. and we can head out to the airport afterward. Sound okay with everyone?"

"Yea."

"Great."

"Fine with me."

"Yes." Henry was hardly able to think about another meal. He sipped his water.

A sad cloud hung over the table. Dismal faces reflected dismal spirits. No one expected the tour to be festive, but the obvious reality of their insights caused a downturn. A deep breath was drawn. A heavy sigh was released. Another drink was sipped.

"Would it be safe to speculate that stations at Arizona and California are experiencing the same situations?" Ingrid voiced her wonderings out loud.

"No doubt." It was Will. "I mean what we've learned so far is the same information that we've been reading in Reuters and seeing on CNN. It's just that we now have seen it with our own eyes. Touched it! Sounds to me like the United States border condition is a grossly negative function of the poverty and corruption in some Central American countries," Will stated.

Ingrid resettled in her seat and dabbed her lips with a napkin. She averted anyone's eyes by wiping droplets from her water glass.

"We knew that." Zigmund offered his opinion on the matter.

"I realize that we're not going to change the condition. I just keep wondering what the agents and guards think. You know, what they see as needing improvement and what might be most helpful." Henry was digging beneath the surface.

"We're not expected to solve the border problems. We were already aware that the outcome of separation, of delays, of the conditions, would be detrimental for the seekers." Zigmund continued.

A break in the comments lasted for a few beats before Stuart spoke. "You're right. We knew there was trauma knotted up in the immigrant situation. We now have our first-person experiences to urge us forward, and I'm hoping we can bring some attention that may result in humane advances. My written document involving this encounter will be ready whenever I can get on a docket for an upcoming committee hearing."

Stuart picked up his eyeglasses and settled them on his face. He brushed a crumb off his trousers and look over the faces of the others. "I'm about set. Everybody ready to go?" He prodded the tired group. They rambled back once again to the rented minivan that was now covered with red dust half-way up on every side.

TWENTY-ONE

A parking lot without a vacant space greeted the group when they returned to the hotel. Stuart circled the lot and stalked the slots with cars from out of town that were kissed with the red earth of the land. He settled on a spot across the median from their lodging and apologized for the inconvenience of having to walk. Ingrid and Sarah were out and ahead of the rest half-way to the entrance, chatting and gesturing with Will and Stuart talking behind them. Zigmund was in front of Henry when he spoke.

"Quite a day, mm?"

"Yes."

"I believe I may take a sit in the hot tub to relax."

"Not a bad idea. I'm not ready to go inside yet." Henry entertained the soothing notion of a quiet walk.

"You go on. I'll see you in the morning." Zigmund headed toward the entrance in no hurry.

The dry night air was still warm, and the breeze was non-refreshing. In the distance the sound of howling coyotes rose above the thirty-foot wooden plank wall that spanned miles of hot, level, Texas plain. Dust swirled in a lazy response as vehicles stopped and started at intersections and between brick structures. Darkness hung over Henry and engulfed the camp back where a few thousand people slept, blanketed in mylar and uncertainty.

Two women carrying packages moved through an alleyway in the shadow of a rising moon. The hotel was the tallest building in the area, but other establishments were noisy and brightly doing business A light wind was still pushing between the structures, yet relief from the heat was hours off. Warmth hugged Henry's body like an unneeded blanket and he welcomed the touch of moving air.

He walked in an opposite direction of the women, wrestling to get his bearings, and sorting out considerations of the day. He moved puzzling over the aberrations that created this stretching city. His questions centered first on the geography and what lay beyond the four directions, and how the boundaries came to exist. The evolving occupations and livelihood of the area; farming, manufacturing, airports, then immigrants were results of progress. He recognized the need of governance and the necessity for peripheries and how they required acceptance of authority. At the forefront of his mind was psychological training grappling with visuals of huddled humanity who were sequentially harboring physical injury and sustaining mental damage. All these areas mingled while Henry sauntered over dirty stone sidewalks and across sticky asphalt roads.

The tornado of concerns blew his deliberations to Francisco and Verdi. He expected that, eventually, the child would accept the arms of his mother. Perhaps not today but then again, maybe so. It would be a question of when rather than if. He chafed over the reality that this mother would never forget the ache she suffered from the disdain of her child. He worried that the mother would hurt every bit as much as the child *because* the child hurt. His contemplation slipped further to multiply this one tragic story by the hundreds of thousands of lives touched by the border.

The aftermath of his mind storm found him not surprisingly back to his experience with Mateo. The boy's face was a distinct image that recurred. It faded and returned with the tones of his despairing mother's voice like a soundtrack. The heart wrenching story of their life's tragedy amounted to more than they should have to endure. Henry's shoulders slumped with the burden of their pain along with his wish to somehow be of help. Amid all the suffering that surrounded him in this city, he felt a need of repentance for his many 'taken-for-granted' blessings. He did not deserve his miracles, and these immigrants didn't deserve their disasters. How could he level the disparity?

Walking had begun to physically deplete him, but his firing brain would not desist. He ambled back toward the hotel. Each step was slower than the last. His tired bones harbored a guarded prospect of rest. When he reached his room, there was little spring in his step and his feet shuffled across the threshold and onto the carpeted floor. The hotel room waited with the sweet bed offering its promise of solace.

His rumpled pants would hardly change appearance as he dropped on the bed. Disregarding clothing and shoes, he lay fully dressed on top of the covers that topped the mattress. He shut his worn-out eyes, but his mind saw hundreds of sobbing mothers and crying children. Arms stretched from one side of a chain link barrier to someone out of reach on the other side. The unpleasant sound of their desperate weeping swirled inside his brain until it morphed into an eerie music played on an out-of-tune piano. It was a haunting bit of notes strung together with sharps and flats and squeaks between. An image of a bony woman with skeletal hands sat at the upright, and as she played, a young boy twirled next to the bench where her fingers touched the ivory keys.

Henry yanked opened his eyes before his mind could trick him into believing who those people were. His memories of Marie and of Dimi would not be diminished by the morbid specters coming through his depressed feelings. For a time, he sat up and stared at the walls in the room with complementary pictures that were intended to soothe and promote calm. Standard, colorful, framed. Probably bolted behind to prohibit theft.

He focused on his gray, soft-sided suitcase lying closed on a stand. The ordinary contents were checked off an imaginary list to distract his thoughts and engage his concentration; four pairs of briefs, two pair of dark socks, two pair of white socks, four white t-shirts, hankies, pajamas, razor, toothpaste, toothbrush, comb, deodorant, bug spray, nail clippers. Next, he forced his attention to the lesson he would have presented to his Cognitive Psychology class that day. He nudged his lagging memory toward the theories, the research systems, the statistical equations that would have been relevant to the material. Emily's question in developmental psych class about how experiences influence our life was an appropriate applied concept for the emotional day he had just spent. Certainly, the experiences of everyone at the McAllen station tonight, last year, and next month would be an unshakeable influence. Undoubtedly, the fear, anxiety, and confusion of the children at the center would surface at times to cause them distress and maybe even nightmares. Who could tell what might trigger an attack of panic in later years, a chain link fence, a uniform, a cement floor, or a silver blanket?

Henry attempted an informal relaxation technique that sometimes helped. Sitting on the bed's edge stretching out his limbs, he flexed the muscles within. A few repetitions left him sleepy but still bombarded with ghosts from the day. He begrudgingly sat up and fluffed the pillow behind him. His eyelids blocked out only the darkness. Inside his head there was a vivid Ferris Wheel, and each cab was swaying with a perplexing dilemma. As the wheel circled, another example of human hardship emerged. Each urgent. Each demanding consideration.

Henry grabbed the TV remote to turn on the set but was not invested in what might be playing. Futile clicking was followed swiftly by the off button. His drowsy body moved out of the bed and went to the bathroom for a splash of cold water. He doggedly walked to the window and opened the curtain to peer out.

The night lights of McAllen were as busy as fireflies. Traffic was hustling in every direction and the bars and restaurants were signaling customers to pull up and come inside. From his window he saw the ability to spend money, to gather with friends, and to walk around freely. Freely. That was it. We had it. They wanted some too. Simple.

The double standard screamed with clarity and he heard it, saw it, felt it. It had been the kind of day that makes an impression that would not leave a person. A memory you absorb in every cell yet would have trouble trying to describe. It reminded him of stumbling on a narrow wooden gangplank and watching the ominous black water open to swallow him. He shook his head to expel the shudder.

He moved slowly between closet, bathroom, and bed. He exhaled deeply and let his shoulders fall. A minute escaped before his curled hand ran over the top of his head and flattened the thinning hair there. He rose again from the bed and ambled to his soft-sided suitcase where the zipper was not drawn closed and opened the luggage. A round, red shape rested in a corner surrounded by socks. Henry picked up the ball that had stowed away amid the essentials. White underwear, plain socks, white handkerchiefs, and a red ball. An unwitting contrast.

Henry squeezed the ball as he always did; a gentle reminder of the pleasure of playing toss with his sweet grandson. Henry held the ball, returned to his bed, and crawled under the blanket. For a time, he lay motionless in the warmth of the covers and stared ahead. Concerns now were obscure and distant without true content. He wanted to be alone, in his room, in his bed, with the blanket, and Dimi's rubber ball.

His head rested deep into the pillow. This time he had doffed his shoes, socks, and pants. His arms and legs were heavy like branches of a Sequoyah, his entire body lethargic, his eyes closed, and his mind drifted unrestrained. At last, he was asleep and floating off to a corner of space free from questions or answers, where souls were visible, and insides were out. The pleasant melodies rose, fell, and rose again, braising a light scent of richly intoxicating serenity.

Henry succumbed to the cherished sleep he desperately needed. Deeper and further his mind wafted until he met total unconsciousness and the gratitude of relief.

TWENTY-TWO

Stuart Samson woke, shaved, showered, and dressed before he noticed the flashing red button on his hotel room phone. He listened to the message. Years of public service, years of military service, and years of working with people, and still, there was no predicting people's behavior. He fastened on his watch, checked his back pocket for his wallet, and made his way to the lobby where the others were waiting for their breakfast with Hugh Gallwith.

"Good morning." Stuart greeted everyone with a smile. He rubbed his hands together in a gesture of anticipation. "Shall we get some breakfast?"

"Henry isn't here," Sarah informed him.

"Oh yes. Well, he isn't joining us this morning. Asked if he might get a pass. Will meet us at the airport. Rough night I think." With that he extended his arm in the direction of the exit.

Morning clocks launched hustling individuals heading off to work in all directions. Yellow buses filled with giggles and wiggles straddled around corners on route to schools with waiting classrooms. By the time his friends were driving to "Sweet Temptations" restaurant, Henry had contacted Sergeant Basil Cayne and been admitted into the processing center on Ursula. Even though Sergeant Cayne was being cordial, Henry sensed the man did not appreciate his showing up. The sergeant handed Henry off to

Agent Santiago with a warning of a strict and brief time limit.

Yesterday, when he visited the cages, he observed that some of the children's faces conveyed fear; there was the same palpable sense of confusion. Along with a few young ones who were whimpering, the voices of a few others rose in supplication. Perhaps the more chilling were the ones who simply sat in silence; withdrawn, staring, sullen. These children had been separated from family or guardians long enough to know that this was another day in a string of lonely, solitary days and they were helpless.

In the boys' quadrant, Henry recognized the child who had cried the day before. Today he was dressed in clean clothes, wide eyed and satisfied to suck his thumb from his mattress. Henry asked why a child so young was separated from his parent, knowing it was not protocol. Agent Santiago explained. "He was found alone near the riverbank yesterday. We arranged for him to be moved to a child welfare location very soon. Excuse me." She was off in another direction.

Alongside Julio was Mateo whom Henry had wanted to see since their contact the day prior. As if sharing the same idea, Mateo was at the mesh, standing and watching. Large dark eyes peered out under uneven strands of thick black hair and small fingers wound around the metal wiring. The child was thin. There wasn't much more to him than the enormous eyes and tousle of hair. His shorts were baggy, and his feet clad with canvas shoes that were also too large.

"Hola, Mateo." Henry spoke softly, keeping a fair distance.

"Hola, Enri."

Henry's heart smiled. He had looked up a few Spanish words to use.

"¿Como esta?" He knew it meant how are you.

"Triste."

Henry did not have a clue. He remembered 'muy bien,' very good, but would be foolish to expect that answer. He repeated what the boy said. "Triste."

"Si, extrano a mi familia."

Henry caught the 'yes' and 'my family' but what was extrano? Under the circumstances it sounded like extract. Nonetheless, it was about his family. He could fill in the blank.

"Si." Henry offered.

"Se llevaron a mi madre." Again, he recognized 'my mother.' Henry tried to silently repeat it so he could look it up later. At least the child was talking.

"Si." Henry tried to keep the conversation moving. It was all he could offer. "Si."

"No se si ella está bien. Y mi padre está herido." The boy looked to Henry with urgency filling his deep eyes. It left Henry with inadequacy growing within.

"Me temo que." Mateo's head bent toward his feet.

"Si, niño. I'm sorry for you." He hoped the message worked its way through the mesh that was a language barrier.

There was no answer from the child. He remained with head lowered. Henry became an intruder on personal anguish. The struggle to stay or leave played out in his mind. His feet had the urge to move on, but his heart wanted to stay and help. There were no directions for helping, no playbook at this point. His efforts were a stab in the dark at best and a stab in the boy's soul at worst. In the end, he chose to let the boy be with his pain, not trying to interfere where he could not be of use. He walked all the way to the exit. While slipping hands into his pockets, he came upon the red ball. He took it out and bounced it without thinking. Suddenly, he came to a halt with the first idea that had made sense in two days. He hurried to Mateo's enclosure and held up the red ball. Mateo looked at Henry, the ball, and a weak wave of recognition crossed his face.

At first, Henry was going to just give it to him. He got a better idea.

"Mateo, ball?" Henry held out the round object to help the translation.

"Pelota." The boy was sitting on his mattress. He leaned forward and nodded. *"Pelota."*

"Color, red." Henry pointed repeatedly at the ball.

"El color es rojo."

"Rojo. Red." Henry nodded his head and said the words again.

"Red?" Mateo made a meek attempt.

"Si, red. Rojo. Si." Henry cheered.

Henry's fingers circled the ball twice around. "Round." He made the gesture again.

"Redondo." Mateo made a circular motion. He slid off the mattress and came back to the mesh.

"Redondo. Round." Henry repeated the words and nodded toward the child.

"*Redondo*. Round."

Henry let the ball hit the floor then he caught it. He dropped the ball and caught it again. "Bounce."

"Rebotar."

"Rebotar. Bounce." By this time, Henry was tinged with encouragement. He bounced the ball and said the Spanish words for ball, round, and bounce once, twice, and three times. His joy spread to Mateo and on to a few others. He watched as little Julio kicked his legs back and forth on his cushion. His thumb sucking slurped in rhythm with his legs.

"Wait right here," Henry instructed as he scurried to one of the agents attending to someone near the latrines. He asked if it would be permitted if he gave the ball to the child. There was hesitation. The man explained the disruption if one child had a toy and the others did not. There was also the possibility the child might *eat* the toy. And finally, the guard stated that it would be unfortunate if, in any way, a child was hurt, even unintentionally, due to the object in question.

With evident exasperation, Henry returned to the cell. In his worst Spanish interpretation, he told Mateo. "I can't give you *rojo pelota*. I'm so sorry."

"La pelota rojo es tuya," Mateo agreed.

Henry slipped the ball into his pocket and followed with his hands. His eyes lingered on Mateo. He wanted to say so much more. The child had seen more than a seven-year-old should.

"Adios."

"Adios." Henry left the building.

Outside, a wisp of warm air brushed against his withered skin. The sky was coming alive with the vibrant sun's creative color scheme. Butter yellow melted into juicy orange and contrasted the deep blue hue that was as pretty a picture as the yellow rose of Texas itself. Henry paused a moment to let his aching eyes adjust. The pleasant panorama tempered his cheerless mood, and he allowed himself a tentative smile when considering that he conversed with the boy, sort of. Maybe, a bit.

He made his way on foot from the processing center to the new tent structures miles away and found that it took much longer than the drive yesterday. Henry needed the time to let his thinking fall into place and to shake his caffeine blast. The three cups of coffee had hyped him up and not yet worn off.

A crunch beneath his foot was an alert to an encounter with a Texas cockroach. Henry stopped, squatted, and observed the crushed bug. It wasn't as big as many had boasted. It wasn't a foot long. Still, the collision proved unsettling because the queasy sensation irritated him right through his shoe. Still squatting, he noticed several other of the menacing insects scurrying around under the veil of damp shade from a live oak. A shudder traveled under his shirt, and he wondered what other various critters that had been highlighted in his information packet he might encounter. He rose and let his hands slip into the safety of his trouser pockets.

He meandered along the parched road parallel to the expansive border wall. Palm leaves swayed lightly atop the tall trees. More cacti menaced alongside. The thorns were painful warnings of certain damage if encountered. Henry steered clear. The air was warm, and the breeze had a humid heft as it blew in off the Grand River. The morning sun brightened objects on the ground with an alarmingly blinding sheen.

The farther he walked from the border station, the more the noises took up the familiarity of city life. Drifting scents teased his nose with the distinct aroma of morning tortillas. Workers leaving home for another day on the job. Shoppers, teens, grandparents, all had their reasons for being out on the streets of their hometown. Motorcycles roared past and horns honked at crowded intersections. The enormous processing station was shrinking behind him.

Henry did not have to check the time to know the group was enjoying breakfast and Hugh Gallwith's southern drawl. He couldn't make himself move more quickly. His shoes were filled with the heaviness that had spilled from the facts in his head and influenced the weight on his shoulders till it ended up at his feet. It would have to be okay that he missed out.

A watchful agent met him at the entrance, having been alerted by the sector chief, and warned him of protocol and time constraints. This day he was directed to empty his pockets, submit to a hand pat and wand search then ushered through a metal detector. Henry posed no threat. He stepped inside the enormous tent with a strange feeling of familiarity even though he had only spent a short time there the day before. Perhaps it was the anticipation that encouraged him.

There was a rhythmic sound that Henry picked up on and he made his way through the vastness to where it grew more distinct. In a shadowed corner, rocking a small young boy, a female social worker smiled out at him from inside an enclosure. The rocking chair offered up a cadence as it swung forward and back on the flat cement floor. Henry nodded to the woman and the sleeping child and raised his finger to his lips.

Henry concentrated a bit and realized that things had changed. Several new faces occupied the enclosures, and he couldn't remember where his group had found Rosa. He walked slowly down the aisle, peering into each section, trying not to impose, but failing. Many of the women had similar features; their hair was dark, eyes were dark, clothes a little tattered from a grueling dusty trip. When a few minutes had passed, Henry spoke in his pitiful attempt at the language.

"¿Rosa? ¿Dónde está Rosa?" What he said sounded like 'don't, day yes tar Roza.' He got no response. He continued down the outside aisle on one side and up the other of the massive tent structure. Where Rosa Elmar had been the day before now lodged several different women with children. Henry looked into their faces and over their heads. He stood on his toes. He hurried around the fencing. When he had doubled back and repeated his steps without any success, he questioned the agent nearby.

Henry explained his concern, described the woman, gave what details he remembered. The agent keyed open an iPad and ran his arrow across the column until Elmar, Rosa, appeared next to the date, May 2, 2018.

"She got her tear sheet, was released last night."

"What? How? When last night?" Henry's voice was louder than he meant it to be.

"Sorry, sir. That's all I can say."

"Well, was she deported? Her son is still here. There's been a mistake. Her son is still here," even louder.

"Sir, I don't have the details. I'm sorry. She got her sheet. She was released. That's all I know."

"Well, who can I ask?" Henry attempted to calm his voice.

"Sir, I'm sorry."

"Okay, okay. If she was released, from your experience, where do you think she might go?"

"Well, sir, I wasn't here when she left. But maybe she was released until the second interview. If that's the case, she would have been asked to stay around until that date is set."

"We have to find her. We must tell someone. Her son is still in the McAllen processing center. He needs her. How can we locate her?"

"I'm sorry, sir, but I can't help you. The processing agents know what they're doing."

Henry waved his hand. He felt mocked and dismissed, did a three-sixty, looked again into the enclosure for reassurance. She still wasn't there.

"I need to contact sector chief Sergeant Basil Cayne. Can you help me with that? Just a phone call," Henry implored.

"This way."

He stepped quickly while agitation festered inside with a growing determination to somehow intervene. He needed to think. Individuals nearby were assuring him that they would investigate the matter. The words bounced off his ears without the slightest register. He sensed the others were not as upset as he was, and their interest fell short of a personal level and even less urgent.

Sergeant Cayne could not be reached. Henry stomped through the hall and out the door. Exasperation buoyed him along as he tried again to center himself and comprehend what had happened and what needed to happen next.

Where could Rosa have gone? How far could she travel since last night? Would she have waited for her boy? What, if anything, could *he* do? Where would he begin? The questions swirled unanswered in his mind.

Outside of the enormous tent were a few groups of women classified as 'head of household.' It meant they were without a man but with at least one child. They clustered in small familial groups. They used the ground as a seat or a bench for a change table. Conversation was minimal because the people were united by grief and struggle, but they didn't know each other. They had suffered and overcome so much, but their common ground was simply the ground. They left their old ground for this new ground. They counted on this new ground to sustain them.

Henry spied a bench and walked toward it. There were women sitting there, but an inch of unoccupied space at the end assured him there was enough room for himself. He inhaled a long breath and exhaled a truckload of exasperation. His back hit the metal just as his head lowered to his chest. He succumbed to the fatigue and welcomed the easy place just beyond it. Exhaustion drew him to doze and temporarily relieved him of the burden of concern.

Henry's musings settled on the seven-year-old boy he had left not long before. They twisted and wrenched until torments poked from the other side of awareness. It was not much of a leap for him to next encounter visions of his grandson and struggle with worry for Dimi. His fingers twitched on the bench as pictures of Anelia and Josef crossed paths with his memory of Marie. He woke with concern for his clients and their adjustment to his absence. He wondered how his classes were going for his substitute. He sank into siesta again.

TWENTY-THREE

Spring was beginning to appear on the campus of the University of Virginia as evidenced by warmer temperatures, intense pace of the classwork, and more couples paired up on the greening lawns of the mall. Library halls bustled with students rushing to complete research, to finalize theories, and to notate sources. Final exams would be around the corner followed shortly by degree ceremonies. It was an amalgam of pressure and spring fever.

Jamison Corlander would have enough credits to complete his bachelor's degree in December if he stayed on track. That meant that he had assignments to complete, final exams to study for, and football workouts to attend. Stress in his life was on the same par as most of the students around him except for that one other thing. The one aspect of his life that was uber-stressful and messed with his head. That one thing that didn't make any sense no matter what lens he looked through. The thing that he thought about between every other thought he had.

In the middle of an econ lecture, his mind would drift off to a scene with him and Cilla embracing in front of a fire. Walking into the gym, he could smell her scent above the sweat and stinky shoes that permeated the air. When he left campus, the idea of her delicate skin transformed the steering wheel into something soft and sensual. Try as he might, he suffered through each class with her, desperately straining to take notes while staring through the words in the textbook. If he looked up at her at the front of the room, his heart raced. The situation was crazy; crazy exciting, crazy fun, crazy wrong on so many levels.

During the rare moment when he was actually concentrating on academics or sports, his questions mounted about the future. A degree in Economics with a minor in Psychology was an impressive beginning for an athletically talented Native American young man. But, then what? The curriculum advisor had spent time talking to him and testing to see what jobs would suit him. There were tests of personal interest, aptitude, specific ability, and more. There were papers from recruiters looking for graduates from his program and the ever-present athletic scouts.

Much celebrated and mutually disappointing job fairs were sponsored every year, available to the student body, but semi-productive. So many possibilities were advertised with vendors. Booths were manned by the most outgoing and congenial of representatives. Each gave the impression of interest for every candidate that approached but, in the end, competition was fierce, and qualifications were demanding.

Jamison could see the dwindling days of study leading to the endless unfolding years of work. He wanted to be certain that he chose well. He wanted the employer and the employee to have a mutual respect and a rewarding experience. He didn't want to mess up and, honestly, some of the decisions he was making lately were worrisome.

The first choice, if he could be allowed to dream, would be to play pro football. Anywhere, any team, just be a professional. He grew up watching the Redskins. With all the references to Native Americans, he still loved the team; maybe even more because of it. If not Washington, there were several runners-up: Green Bay, Dallas, Denver. Or *any* other one. Football was in his physical make-up. He would not deny it got him going in the morning and kept him practicing longer than the other team members.

He was smart enough to know that the dream probably wasn't going to happen, and he needed to do well in school. His chosen field of study was going to open possibilities in the work field, and he was a good student despite his self-doubt. It was a matter of staying on track.

He was flying down the staircase, taking the steps two at a time, after dropping off his three-thousand-word summary for his Advanced Government class. It had taken an incredible amount of library time not to mention his hunt and peck typing technique. The relief formed a grin literally across his entire face. The double doors sprang open as he pushed through them as if pushing through the backfield with the ball tucked under his arm. Sunshine greeted him with an appreciative stir of warm air. He intended to head to the cafeteria before a female voice called, bringing him to a halt. Jamison swiveled at the sound of his name.

"Jamison Corlander, right? You probably don't know me. I'm Sondra Mercer. We have a couple classes together." The sun shone on her springy dark hair giving it a soft glow as it brushed the top of her navy-blue hoody. Even without make-up her hypnotic eyes were fringed with thick lashes. Her smile intrigued him.

"Yes, Sondra. I've seen you in class. Social psych and what else…"

"Inter-macro."

"Oh, sure. Professor 'fun and games.' How ya doin.'"

"I'm good. Sorry to bother you, were you off to class?"

"No, no. S'up?"

"Well, I was just talkin' to my friend, Brindi, an' we can't remember what time the final is on Monday. I can't find my syllabus an' she was sure it was at 9:00, but I didn't think so. Do you remember?"

"Yea, it's at 9:00."

"Okay." Sondra did not take her soft eyes off him.

"Are you ready for it? I've got some serious studying to do for sure."

"No way am I ready. There's a study group tomorrow night at the Beta house," she spoke it as an invitation.

"Really? Is there room for one more? I gotta' pass this." Jamison was literally willing to take any help he could find.

"Sure. Come around 7:00. Bring food. It might be a long night."

"Well great. Thanks. See ya." Politely, he waited as she walked in front of him. He steered himself toward the cafeteria. Despite the image of Dr. Fletcher Price, fun-and-games, and the upcoming intermediate macroeconomics exam, he allowed himself to enjoy the pleasure of daylight in the invigorating afternoon air.

Food was an uncomplicated pleasure for the growing young athlete who depended on fuel to maintain his game. He kept his menu distributed with appropriate amounts of nutrients, carbs, and protein. When it sustained his strength, he was satisfied. If it tasted good that was a bonus.

Jamison went through the cafeteria line, picking up what he needed from his calorie intake. His calendar for the next few days drifted through his mind. He considered the classes and deadlines mixed in with the workouts. A pang of dread clanged in his head just as he bit into a chicken salad sandwich loaded with grizzle. The idea of a study group always appealed in the beginning, but sometimes it wasn't as helpful as it might be. He needed someone else's take on the statistics in inter-macro, but he didn't have the luxury of wasting time. There was the quiz his Fiscal Accounting professor threatened with. There was that girl again, springy hair, blue hoody, walking through the cafeteria and out the door to the hall.

She has the prettiest caramel skin, and she wears her blue jeans rather good! The sturdy athlete battled with the grizzle in his sandwich, devoured his potatoes, green beans, and apple, before downing two cafeteria size cartons of whole milk. He barely looked up from his tray as dozens of students shuffled in and out of the eatery; some finishing a meal, some starting one, and others cutting through as a shortcut to a more important destination. Life on campus was replete with crunch times, crazy times, boring times, and life-altering times. There was no lack of opportunity to engage in group adventures that were wildly exciting and equally dodgy. Like the time his buddies had duct taped the kicker to the goal post after practice. He had eagerly joined in without a second thought. Or the time five of his friends cajoled him into helping them lift the linebacker coach's VW and leave it sideways in the stadium entrance.

Truly his focus was football, and he admitted it was demanding on his time and stamina. In addition, was this whole crazy *thing* with a professor, twice his age, out of his league; and with that disturbing realization, his phone rang. It was her.

"Hey."

"Jamison, can you talk?" Priscilla's voice could be sultry even if she were describing an oil change.

"Yea, what's up?"

"It's been a few days since we studied together. How about we set a time for tomorrow evening?"

Her voice conjured up images of her curvy body stretched out next to him. It was an energetic warmth that eased through his muscles and made his joints weak. The taste of his lunch, the concept of football practice, and the idea of anything else was easily erased from his mind.

"I really need to study with you…but I can't tomorrow. I'm goin' to a study group for my inter-macro exam an' I gotta' nail it. It's a tough course."

"Mm."

"Got any other study times open?"

"I'll have to get back to you."

Jamison heard the click and wondered if Professor Priscilla Harris-Hunt was pissed. It was the first time he could not accommodate her schedule. He made a point to be as available as possible when she called. How she might take a 'no' was going to be a revelation to him; hopefully, not too harrowing. She had definite ways of getting her feelings across; positive and negative. Without time to ponder this dilemma further, he grabbed his tray and disposed of it.

Striding out the door and back into the daylight, he continued across the paved lane where bodies and clamor greeted him on all sides. Students with frisbees, some bikes, a skateboarder, and clumps of chatting young adults reverberated relief and worry in equal turns. Several paces farther, he noticed Sondra Mercer sitting on a bench with a textbook open on her lap. She obviously did not see him, and he chose not to interrupt her by saying something. He maintained his pace until he passed where she sat and continued to head toward the lockers and work-out room. A few more steps felt safe before he could steal a quick look back toward her direction, but she was gone.

TWENTY-FOUR

The Beta house was a three-story structure nearly two centuries old with modest gray siding and black shutters. The front door was a contrasting solid, sky-blue-pink with a more recent door knocker made of copper and resembling a smiling lion. The sloping front porch had several assorted dismal wicker chairs of various pink hues spread across its wooden planks and an actual thriving fern suspended from a linked chain at the overhang.

Jamison could hear female voices when he reached the front walk. He did not use the smiling lion to knock, rather made a fist and pounded. It was futile. He tried the doorknob, and opened the door just before saying, "Hey," with sufficient volume. All chattering halted, and everyone looked toward the tall, handsome, guy standing sheepishly in the doorway.

"Uh, hi?" He held up a pizza box and smiled weakly. Hoping for someone to acknowledge him, or anyone to cut through the awkward silence, he questioned, "Inter-macro, study group?"

The females continued to stare at the hot dude from the football team, a tight end with a tight end. Jamison was puzzled at what might be going through their heads. One girl had her mouth open. Eventually, one senior sitting on the couch at the left side of the room gestured.

"Sondra's group. End of the hall. Last room on the right."

Her eyes followed him as he moved uncomfortably through the middle of the gathering. Jamison was agile, but the paces between the girls were excruciatingly awkward, and he felt like a giant among fluttering fairies. Once he was past them and out of the room, the wood floored hallway squeaked with his every step. The corridor was narrow and brief. In the last room on the right were two young women with notebooks and pens, a tray of cheesy nachos, several cans of soda in an ice chest, a TV with the sound muted, and on the left Sondra Mercer sat on an antique loveseat with her textbook opened on her lap, just as he had last seen her.

"Study group." Partly with a sigh and partly with a query, Jamison moved through the doorway and into the room which served as a sorority receiving room. Its ceiling was high, the walls were paint over wallpaper in a soft cream color, and the curtains were delicately faded print of nineteenth century headwear: top hats and ladies' bonnets. Two fuchsia-colored chairs were occupied by Maris and Brindi, who Sondra introduced. The only available seat was next to Sondra, and it looked a little tight. Jamison stepped in and dropped to the floor in front of the loveseat. He stretched his legs across the Moroccan print area rug and placed his veggie pizza next to the nachos.

"Erik Steffen might show up. Know him?"

"Uh."

He slipped his book from the weather worn back-pack that had served him for two-thirds of his university experience. The bag from the first third had belonged to his brother who had completed his college education a year before Jamison began. The wear on that hand-me-down backpack had been obvious, but the tradition of handing down was strong. For him, accepting the burden as well as the strength within the edges of the pack was as if he were donning the breastplate his brother wore in battle. The battle of learning, striving, achieving, and sometimes even failure, was received as a gift; for with it all came knowledge. Customs in his Powhatan culture were strong, and beliefs were honored in his family. Even now, the only reason he did not continue to use the bag that his brother used was the stitching had become so tattered that he wanted to preserve what was left to avoid complete ruin.

Fishing for a pen, he came up with a highlighter of bright green instead. Quickly, Sondra leaned over his shoulder and offered a Bic. The act was so swift, Jamison had hardly enough time to take a second swipe in the creases of his satchel. He intended to thank her with a marginal smile on his face when he noticed her almond eyes, dark beneath a fringe of lashes, staring intently at him. The shock of her gaze and the nearness of her knee at his shoulder sent a little uncomfortable blast up his arm. Her fingers pressed his as he reached for the pen, and they lingered along his knuckles a heartbeat longer than necessary. Her lips parted into a cheery smile and the almond eyes giggled at him from under the canopy of lashes.

Sondra attempted to bring Jamison up to speed about what the three girls had discussed thus far. It didn't take long for academics to prevail, and the foursome centered their attention to the upcoming final exam. Among them, they offered possible test questions, checked each other on equations, reviewed former quizzes, and assessed passages in the text that were highlighted during lectures. Jamison was relieved that the females were serious, that no one dissolved into giggles or even worse, gossip. An appropriate chuckle about the material or Professor 'fun and games' surfaced here or there from the girls and he even found himself laughing a time or two.

He gained insight into some of the tough areas that had bogged him down while unchecked time passed. When Brindi said that she had to make a late library run, Jamison rose to leave as well. Encouragement replaced dread about his prospects for the upcoming test. The study session had been beneficial, and he told them he was glad he came. He thanked Sondra for the invitation.

"Let me walk you out," she offered as she rose from the loveseat. "Ugh." She moaned softly and stretched her denim clad legs. Slipping in front of Jamison, she led him through the squeaky hallway, the now quiet front room with only two co-eds watching a movie, and onto the wooden porch.

Stars in the sable sky shone like far off spotlights. The air was cool after a warm spring day, and the essence of anticipation was nearly palpable. Blossoms were peeking from young branches, students were preparing for launch, couples were coupling up, and the eager expectancy was keen.

The friction of bursting spring fever was poking Jamison outside and in. What's more, he sensed that Sondra felt something too. He faced her to say thanks once more and realized she had stopped on a step that left her eye level with him. Before he formed words, she spoke. "I'm glad you came." Her voice dipped in sugar; her smile even sweeter. Perfect eyebrows arched above the thick lashes that batted over soft brown eyes. Her gaze was captivating. He sensed an anticipation in her expression. If he didn't analyze it, he felt something too, wanted this something to happen. His brain contemplated a second too long. She brushed a kiss against his lips.

He didn't push her away, nor did he ask for it to stop. What he did do was stand still without kissing her back, like a wooden totem pole. *What a jerk.* A scorn of self-derision snaked up from his ankles to his Adam's apple, and he criticized himself inwardly. It was a kiss, an innocent kiss. He could have appreciated it. Now he had hurt Sondra's feelings in a way that was edged with embarrassment; his and hers. She dropped those almond eyes.

"I'm sorry…" he tried to say, but she shook her head and his comment fell to the ground.

"No. It's okay. I should apologize." Her voice remained sweet.

"I, I…" he stammered with nowhere for the words to go.

"Do you have someone?" It was a fair question. How should he answer?

"Kinda'…" *Did he have someone? Did someone have him? Was there a mutual…*what? Love? Interest? Lust? Is there a term for 'not-friends with benefits?' Were he and his professor beneficial? It was a puzzlement, and he always ended up at the same dead-end when he questioned the situation.

"Listen, I'm really glad you asked me to come. It helped a lot. You and your friends are brilliant. Maybe we can get together another time." It was lame. He knew it, and he knew she knew it. With a spontaneous movement, he gently pulled on one of her springy curls. He smiled genuinely at her beautiful face and coaxed a grin out of her.

Knowing that saying more would probably make things worse, he remained silent as he hoisted the backpack over his shoulder and walked to the road. For a moment he entertained the idea of a half-turn to wave back at her but instead kept moving. He would have seen her watching him take each step with his long legs, flex each muscle in his back and arms, notice the air ruffle his blue-black hair, until the night melded with his shadow and he was out of her sight. Then he would have seen her stand and watch a little while longer.

TWENTY-FIVE

Sondra Mercer walked through the corridor in Gilmer Hall at the University of Virginia so many times that she felt like part of the staff. Not the custodial staff. Not the professional staff. Somewhere in between, the student staff, if that were ever a thing. She had no desire to become a professional student. That was not her game. Her intent centered on a degree, a career, and UV in the rearview mirror.

She was in her fourth academic year. She went to her share of parties, but she wasn't a boozer. There were lots of getting-to-know-you opportunities, but no real serious relationships developed. Some girlfriends were trustworthy, but she learned which from experiencing the opposite too many times to count. Her GPA was decent, and she had her head on straight.

Sondra had a good grasp of self-awareness with a plan for where she was going and how to get there. Turning twenty-two on campus allowed her to take stock of herself and forced her to look outside of the fortress to the proverbial real world. Her dad would say she was on track. Being a woman in 2018 was easier than in past generations. The prospects were better; not best, but better for females than ever before. She had just enough smarts, just enough ambition, and just enough of a credit score to accomplish her goals.

The day that began cloudy had dropped its morning chill and transformed into a brisk, sunny, afternoon. With two days left of exams for the spring session, students and professors were scurrying. The former to cram and sit for final exams. The latter to oversee final exams, grade, and record them all. It would be a coin flip to say which group wanted the semester to be over most.

Down the hall was the Social Psychology classroom where Professor Harris-Hunt was about to proctor one of her finals. It was odd that the prof was doing her own exam and not having a teacher assistant stand in. Harris-Hunt had a stick up her ass most of the time. Such a bitch, she never changed a grade even if the student begged, cried, or went to the dean. She acted like she owned the department and discovered everything there was to know about psychology. *Hell, maybe she did.*

Jamison Corlander got along with her. He talked to her after class or before. Harris-Hunt was nice to him. She even smiled once when he was saying something to her in the hallway. Guys just had a way; easier. Especially the good-looking ones. Especially the good-looking football players with the ripped abs and bulging arms, the long, dark, hair and the deep black eyes that could drown a female. Jamison Corlander had it all. No wonder Sondra couldn't stop reliving his lips against hers.

Inside the lecture hall, students took their seats, having to leave an empty chair between them because it was the final. Some jerk would inevitably forget the Scantron, or a pencil. The international students had their translators in hand, ready to furiously manipulate the language so they could understand the test questions. Harris-Hunt had her back to the class, arranging some pages on the desk. She moved in a rhythm that caused her bottom to shake beneath her yellow cotton suit. *She's doing that on purpose; there's a guy in the front row.*

Sondra eased into a seat in the last row, up in the back of the room. Because the rows were each raised somewhat above the one before, students in the back looked on the entire scope of the classroom. It allowed for her to stay undisturbed during the final. No one would walk in front of her or excuse themselves to shimmy past. It did make it obvious, however, when others were finished while she toiled on.

When Professor Harris-Hunt addressed the class with the directions for her exam, heads picked up and looked toward her. It was at that precise moment that Jamison Corlander barreled into the room, out of breath, and sweaty, as if he had just run from the football field with a linebacker hanging onto his jersey. He mumbled a curt "sorry" and fell into an aisle seat midway down the steps.

Harris-Hunt made an unpleasant face and explained the parameters of the exam, duration, expected date for posting of grades, and a non-convincing platitude about enjoying everyone this semester. She picked up the stack, counted out enough for each row, and handed them to the student on the east end. It was weird how her fingers deliberately held onto the papers before she let them go into Jamison's hand. And did her hip sway a bit more toward him than the student in the rows before and after his? She was so 'extra.'

The ninety minutes allotted was ample time but as Sondra read each question and thoroughly considered each a, b, and c, the minutes ticked away faster than they should have. With each student getting up to leave, the pressure intensified. There were five students left in the classroom, then there were four. When number three placed the exam on the front desk and left, Sondra saw that only she and Jamison remained working. Professor Harris-Hunt was pouring over what looked like a Psychology journal and did not even look at the completed exams.

The tension won out when she stopped double checking each answer and gathered up her pages and back-pack. She took the steps, leaving her Scantron and exam paper on the front desk. She didn't speak to the professor who had not acknowledged her, or anyone else during the session. Her aim was to wait outside the door for Jamison to come out. Maybe they could talk about the test. Maybe he would invite her for coffee. She did not look his way, knowing he would be out of the room in only a few minutes. The ninety minutes designated were almost up. She didn't have to be anywhere and talking to him was worth waiting a few minutes. It was a relief to have the exam behind her.

Five minutes passed, and the classroom door remained shut. After fifteen minutes, Sondra checked the clock in the next room. It was well past the ninety-minute time allocation. *What was taking so long? There was not another door. What was he doing? Maybe the prof had asked him to help grade or something. No. That would not happen.* She was feeling edgy. Something was bugging her, but she couldn't exactly say what it was. She mentally pieced together a random smattering of puzzle parts. *He had made the prof laugh once. Harris-Hunt had lingered a little bit when handing him the tests.*

Sondra drew close to the classroom door and listened. Because it was a lecture hall, the wood was densely thick to avoid noise. She heard nothing. She gripped the knob, stepped through the small crack she had made, and her eyes fell upon two forms standing precariously close to each other next to the desk where final exams rested. Again, the young man evoked an impish smile from the woman. He was talking in a hushed tone, and Sondra didn't have to hear what was being said. Her feminine instinct caught what was passing between the two figures standing at the bottom of several rows of seats.

In an instant, she realized that she hadn't imagined the lingering finger against his hand, nor the provocative smile in the hallway several days earlier as he stood positioned over the professor like a teenage crush. It all made sense now, unfortunately. He was trapped in her spider's web, and even though he didn't know it, Sondra had a suspicion it wasn't going to end well.

She let the door slam shut and perused the hallway filled with other senior students and psychology majors. There was no haste in her footsteps, but a determination floated through her that overtook her direction. Voices faded into background noise. Was she angry? Jealous? Surprised? Had she suspected this, or was it a case of once you know it you figure you knew it all along? The remarks formed in her head, and by the time she reached the stairs, she had her next move all figured out.

TWENTY-SIX

"Stuart, your phone is ringing again," Ingrid pointed out.

"I'm so sorry." Stuart was accustomed to the inconvenient interruptions but was sensitive to the effect it had on others.

"Go ahead and take the call."

"I'm really sorry." He repeated before he answered the phone. He leaned forward in the terminal seat, bending his head to stifle his voice. His effort didn't work.

"Peter, good morning. Who? Oh, yes. What?... What?... He did WHAT? We're in the airport terminal about to board any minute. What the…did he say why? No way! If this is a joke it isn't funny. I know you don't joke. Okay, what else did he say? All right. No. There's nothing you can do, don't worry. As soon as we hang up, I'm calling Hennesy."

"What is it?" Will Dalton stood next to Stuart who was now standing with smoke exiting through his ears.

"Please excuse me. I have to make a quick call. I'll be right back." Stuart hit a few numbers on his cell and walked away through the wide United Airline corridor. Will looked over to Zigmund who was now standing with pipe in mouth. Sarah and Ingrid exchanged perplexed glances before Sarah rose to her feet and followed Stuart's smoke for a couple yards.

He was still moving. She looked back at the others, and their faces reflected her concern.

"This can't be good. Maybe it's about Henry," she supposed out loud. "I hope he's okay." She returned to where she had been sitting but couldn't make herself bend back onto the bench. The concern that had mounted while waiting for Professor Novak to show up was now transferred to the nature of this upsetting phone conversation.

The people brought together for this unusual excursion were getting to see each other in all sorts of nerve-wracking situations. Sarah fashioned herself as calm in tense situations. Was she upset now? Irritated? Worried? No. *I'm calm.* But the others…

Ingrid was still sitting on the molded seat where she had been. Her boarding pass had captured her attention. Will stood still with thumbs in his belt loops. Sarah assumed he would be good under pressure with no reason to back up that presumption. Zigmund reseated himself with one ankle on the opposite knee and watched the news loop on the TV.

"I hope he gets back here before they call to board." Sarah had to admit she wasn't calm. "I wonder what's going on."

"**Last call for passenger Langston. Passenger Langston please report to United Airline gate fifteen**." A loudspeaker blared. A couple two rows over were kissing and cooing with hands roaming like worms around their bodies. Across the aisle, Sarah could see a mature couple who were not enjoying the pleasure of each other's company. First, he couldn't hear and asked her to repeat. She spoke louder. He disagreed with her. She insulted him. He cursed. They both sat next to each other and looked straight ahead with muffled grumbles.

"Where is Stuart?" she ultimately couldn't hold the question in.

"Give him a minute," Will suggested.

The impression of the older couple crossed her mind. The image caused her to collect herself and return to the bench. *Give him a minute, indeed.*

Sliding her own phone from the innards of her purse, she checked for messages, expecting something from her daughter. It wasn't clear if not hearing from her was any more positive than receiving a demanding message or upsetting text. *Not calm, not calm.*

Stuart finally made his way from the terminal corridor and came to stand in front of the group, wearing his winning smile. He shuffled his shoes a bit before initiating his explanation. "Well," he exhaled demonstratively.

"Yes?" the rest said like backup singers.

"Ha, ha, ha. Apparently, Henry visited the processing center early this morning to see a child he met yesterday, and he walked to the tent camp where we all met the boy's mother. The one who told about her son being killed and her husband being beaten. She had been released last night."

"Oh my. Released last night. Hmm," Ingrid commented.

"Please go on, Stuart," Will encouraged.

"I'm told Henry was upset about the mother being released without the son. He complained, made a little fuss, walked out. Next thing we know, he called his son-in-law because he didn't have my number. His son-in-law called my office and my chief of staff called to let me know that Henry has gone looking for Rosa Elmar. Apparently, Professor Novak made his way through the border gate this morning on his way to Mexico!"

"What the hell? Our plane leaves in less than an hour. What is he thinking?" Will's thumbs went around the leather of his belt when he stepped back three paces before pivoting sideways. "Dammit, Henry!" Various expressions passed across the faces of the four.

Sarah mentally pictured the border crossing bridge with the many brick columns, long covered overhangs, turnstiles, and car lanes. The bustle of the foot and auto traffic was a composite of subdued chaos. It was impossible to know if Henry walked among the throng, but she imagined him out there. Somewhere Henry was mingling among displaced people trying to talk to strangers and failing pitifully at the foreign language. The idea of Henry's inconsiderate behavior gave way to an ounce of respect for doing what needed to be done but acknowledging they would never have dared to do themselves.

TWENTY-SEVEN

Some shoes were designed to comfort the form of a human foot while cushioning the force from the continuous stress that is walking. Other footwear was intended to give a favorable appearance while being tolerated during minimal usage. The force of a single step absorbs the total of a person's body weight. If you walk long enough, repeatedly, the result is fatigue and sore feet.

Henry Novak had crossed the border into Mexico without any more of a plan than that. His intentions were just, but his strategy lacked substance. Determination carried him through day one and most of day two, but by the end of Friday, he realized that he was desperately in need of an improved methodical course. His legs and feet were tired, and the soles of his casual dress shoes were thinned to the point the heat of the sidewalk was burning right through to his socks. There was little doubt he had covered dozens of miles since he left McAllen, Texas.

The rumbling in his stomach sounded loudly even though he didn't feel hungry. At the point of weariness, he chose to nourish his body with food only for energy's sake. He ate once the first day and once the second, feeling adequately full both times. The urgency in his mind kept him from enjoying the meal and the respite. He knew time was not an ally.

Although he didn't come to Texas with much, he left it all behind in a locker at the border. He had his cell phone with him--but that went dead--, and some money for whatever might be necessary. The fog of depression still hung close but that had to end. He had to pull it all together or he wasn't going to make it, let alone find someone.

The search for Rosa Elmar was not only like finding a grain of sugar in an ant hill, but it was also doing so without being able to speak ant. Without an interpreter at his side, his efforts were feeble. Some people feigned ignorance while others outright moved away. He looked different, odd even. His baggy pants, long sleeved shirt, college professor shoes, combined with pale skin and relentless questions, portrayed him in a questionable light of his own unconscious doing.

Across the bridge from Texas, over the Rio Grande, the city of Reynosa, Mexico, had reached its limit with people seeking asylum, people rejected, people ending a journey from a more southern Central American country. Its edges bulged and its innards swelled with masses of humanity coming, going, or waiting. The overflow of Reynosa found its way to the nearby city of Matamoros.

It was here that tent camps pitched in ever increasing rows. Colorful nylon bubbles clustered together just past the river's edge near the Gateway International Bridge. Some dwellings were actual tents. Others were tarps held together with trash bags, sticks, stones, metal rods, or whatever might offer weight. There were hundreds of men, women, and children living in the unhealthy conditions. Two wooden shower stalls erected in the trees were made to suffice for the throngs: with no cleaning supplies. Ten portable toilets had quickly become insufficient as dozens more people arrived every day.

The camps were filled with individuals of all ages trying to make it across the border, stalled for numerous causes. There were those who had made it to the border but had been turned away. Those who had gone before a judge and been sent out to wait. The stories were as varied as the people, yet there was a commonality among them. The experiences of loss, fear, pain, humiliation, depravation, and despair were shared and understood by most. It was a somber atmosphere repeated at most border towns between Mexico and the United States. Still, in the midst were the unpretentious stories of young love cropping up, babies entering the world, and separation being rectified. The latter was what Henry was counting on.

On the beginning of the third day outside of Texas, Henry observed the line form for a meal doled out by Mexican immigration officials. He had witnessed the assembly occur the day before and saw how most of those people received their ration, waited a brief period, and lined up again for the next meal three hours before hand. No doubt because only the first fifty to sixty people received food before the supply ran out.

Henry did not queue up. He had a little money to buy a meal if he wanted one. He sat on a bench next to a young woman and her infant, watching. If Rosa Elmar were in the tent camp, she would need to eat. His expectation was that the likelihood of finding her would increase at the food line. With patient anticipation, he observed everyone until familiar despair seeped in.

When provisions ran out and the crowd dispersed, his view followed a father and son walking toward the river. The son was carrying a long stick while the father carried a plastic bag with what Henry assumed to be worms although he could not know for sure. They made their way toward the water where a few more men were baiting hooks. Others at the river's edge were bathing in the dirty water as the temperature climbed to one hundred degrees Fahrenheit.

When the pair had walked far enough to become specs in the distance, Henry aimed his head toward the sound of slamming car doors. Four women exited a dusty SUV and a man jumped from a pick-up truck. All of them made their way to the back of the truck and lowered the tailgate.

Without so much as a yell to announce their presence, the newly arrived greeted children who had come running. Parents slowly followed the young ones toward the six religious volunteers who had come to deliver necessities. There was bottled water, nutrition bars, individual hand wipes, diapers, feminine items, and soap. As the donors handed out the supplies, they spoke to each person, accepted thanks, offered hope. Henry let the humanitarian activity feed his spirit. He had no way to know that, in a few short months, the number of campers would more than double, and their needs would be overwhelming.

Henry rose from the bench with a slight nod to the young mother. She looked childlike and weathered simultaneously and did not invite conversation. She cradled the baby, he assumed was hers, with a defiant grip. Was the infant moving? Had it moved at all, even once? It hadn't made any sound. Henry swallowed the lump in his throat, and it dropped into the uneasy pit of his stomach. He was past the point of accepting things as they appeared. He entertained the benefit of a doubt, assuming the baby was sleeping, allowing him just enough of a margin to ease out of the muddled circumstance and move away from the bench without further involvement. Along with his suspicion, the moment passed.

He walked by the swarming flies and dreadful smell that emanated from the trees which had become a makeshift bathroom. Human waste, diapers, and female products littered the wooded area and became a flowing sewer when the rain fell. Passing by the expanse caused a queasy unsettling in his empty stomach. Reminders of what was absolutely necessary when lives were reduced to survival, ate through Henry's conscience like termites.

He had talked to many, explaining about Rosa Elmar and her son. He learned a few Spanish words;

no se, I don't know, *no comprende*, I don't understand, and his least favorite, *vete,* go away. He tried to stay gracious and thank each for their time, but his positive attitude was strained. He couldn't shake his need to rectify the mistake. It pushed him when he wanted to stop.

When he encountered a woman, who said she knew Rosa and knew where she was, his enthusiasm flickered. She led him through some grimy paths to a makeshift tent and called to the woman inside. A lady named Rosa, aged, and stooped, emerged from within the tarp and plastic bags. Her hair was gray, her skin was thin, bones were brittle, and she looked at Henry through eyes distorted with cloudy cataracts. The two women waited for Henry to do something, and for a brief time, the three stood silently staring toward each other. Regaining his manners, Henry bowed his head and shook the woman's fragile hand. He offered a smile and attempted 'gracias' in his pitiful accent. Both women nodded back at him. His hand trembled with dissolving excitement as he reached into his back pocket and slipped out his weathered wallet. He extracted some U.S. currency and handed each woman a few bills of small denominations. Others nearby watched the exchange with evident interest. He thanked the aged lady who shared the name and said his good-byes to both women. It was clear he must direct his efforts away from the tent camps.

His plan B was to now try the hospitals. If not for Rosa herself, perhaps for the husband she had described as beaten by the bad men and left behind. There was a sign for Reynosa General Hospital that he had previously seen, so he backtracked to the port city and solicited directions from a young man standing near a store front.

He continually pushed back the unsettling trepidation of danger that surfaced when he turned the corner of a brick building or came up to a rowdy group of teens. His hands hid in worn pockets with the shame of fear while his eyes dared not to make contact. His resilience waned along with confidence in the city that was busy and foreign and frightening. The sting of helplessness was keenly hurtful when a middle-aged woman's cry sought help from across a boulevard. She tussled to keep hold of her purse while a youth twisted and tugged. The battle grew ugly with his pushing the woman until she released the purse, and he ran off too swiftly for anyone to respond. Henry had watched, helplessly, adrenaline rising within him, but his mind overruled the chemical boost. It would have been impossible for him to intervene and the reality saddened his shoulders and diminished his self-esteem.

Ever increasingly slower steps during this last arduous walk found him entering a one-story, stucco building on Bulevar Álvaro Obregón with only a flicker of hope. He waited somewhat patiently for his turn at the reception desk. He was able to make himself understood enough to convey 'Mr. Elmar' and a questioning tone to his voice.

A helpful but overburdened woman looked to her computer screen and scanned the names. She shook her head before the cursor even met the bottom. Henry was persistent.

"Perhaps last week, or the week before," Henry asked.

"*No. No le semana pasada. No, el mes pasado.* Not last week or last month." There was no variation in her voice.

"Gracias."

Henry moved to leave but addressed the woman once more. "Is there another hospital?"

"*Si,* Regional Hospital Del Rio, *y* Hospital Los Lagos, *y* Hospital Esperanza, *y* Las Fuentes, *y* Tierra Santa." She fired them off so quickly, even in English Henry had a difficult time catching the names.

"Are any near here?"

"*Si.* Regional Del Rio is *no* far. I give you directions." She slid a paper and pencil across the counter to Henry, slowly giving him the lefts and rights to this other hospital. He thanked her profusely and departed with a bit more lift in his worn-out shoes.

The sun had seared over Henry and the people out under its merciless rays for this long, dry, day. Now that shadows were forming, the imminent loss of the sun brought dread. Nights posed a confusing dilemma of safety or sleep or neither. His dwindling crunch of bills would not provide him a stay in a decent motel. His credit cards had been maxed out a year before with medical expenses, so interest was all that he could afford to pay. What he could afford now might offer resting on a bed infested with lice or bed bugs. He took his chances outside. He held onto the cash for food or an emergency, expecting no less. Tired from walking, afraid of staying still, he moved in the direction of the other hospital with waning resolve. Mobility was his goal; the pace had slowed. By the time the moon appeared, his search switched to shelter of any type.

Unfamiliar words on buildings offered reminders that he was an outsider. As he moved along, he acutely noticed individuals or small groups huddled under lighted shop fronts. The directions clenched in his palm, his steps pointed according to their instruction, the night sounds worried him into continuous stride. A police car drove by him.

Henry watched the law enforcement cruiser pass and eventually turn into a parking lot far ahead. By the time he arrived at the spot, he was able to discern it was a precinct station. Several other marked cars were parked alongside the building and the light above the door illuminated *"Delegaciones,"* although he didn't understand it was Spanish for precinct other indications were apparent. Allowing for a small amount of security to develop, he crossed the street away from the structure.

Under a sturdy Jacarandas bush, he crouched to sit. The bush's blue flowers were blooming and gently fragrant; seductive and tranquil. Henry sat briefly trying to achieve some relaxation. He checked around for cacti before sprawling out under the silhouette of the police building. The tall palm trees nearby stretched majestically high toward dim stars. Dust mixed with fallen petals combined to obscure the filth of the ground under the night shadows. He lowered his head to his arm, tucked his legs into a fold, and felt the transfer of heat from the baked ground through his clothing. His body lay motionless while his mind fought with facts.

Voices of men floated on the still night air and reached Henry's ears. The sentences bounced back and forth like swift tennis balls on a clay court. The tone suggested irritation, but just when Henry was alarmed enough to sit up, laughter rang out. Ears that were tuned into the banter eventually grew fatigued, his joints yielded, and he dropped down again. He slept but did not rest.

Long since dawn stirred movement in the city, Henry opened his eyes and brushed a mild dew off his cheek. His bones ached and his brain was muddy. The scorpion that had walked beside his rumpled body and stepped across his grimy shoes was long on its way to a more suitable moist area.

The stickiness of soaring temperatures blended with the activity of morning commotion. Launching slowly and growing with a steady rise, the heat and noise increased proportionately. Henry wanted to stay on the ground. He needed more sleep, but begrudgingly rose to an elbow. The police building across the street caught his glance and reminded him where he was. The name of the hospital he was heading for made its way to the clearing portion of his mind. Time was slipping.

He wanted to roll up his sleeves, but sunburn would be an outcome he didn't have time to contend with. A hat would have been a blessing, but there wasn't time for that either, not to mention his meager funds. The directions on the paper twisted like a treasure map. His feeble focus slid him off track repeatedly over the eight and a half miles he needed to cover in order to reach the Regional Hospital Del Rio. It was a draining hike. The distance lengthened with an errant turn at a landmark here, and a misinterpreted sign there, leaving him thirsty and tired when he eventually arrived several hours into the heating day.

The air conditioning was a welcomed greeting as he passed through the double sets of heavy glass doors. He chose a seat and rested for several minutes before continuing to reception. He wanted to wipe the sweat off his hands and face before appearing before the person in authority. It was the least respect he could offer. "Senor Elmar, por favor." He smiled at the young woman as he asked.

She repeated the name and clicked some keys on the keyboard in front of her. She waited. Henry waited. It was scrolling. She shook her head. Henry asked. "*¿Semana pasada* or *mes pasado?*"

The girl clicked more keys and allowed the data to emerge. A moment passed. "*Si.* He was here for two weeks but transferred out last week." Her English was much better than Henry's Spanish.

"Does it say where he went?" Henry was excited to have found a connection but much too worn out to physically show it. The best he could manage was a brief shrug of his shoulders and a long exhale. The young woman provided the name of a nursing home and patiently gave directions. Henry thanked her twice. He gave a little nod with a slight squat that looked more like a curtsy. He would have shaken her hand if she were not across the counter and back to clicking on the keyboard within an instant. A phone rang somewhere behind her.

His spirit was racing outside the door ahead of him even as the blisters on his feet festered. It would be prudent this once to take a taxi, but after waiting several minutes in the heat, he decided to move. He kept his eyes alert to the possibility of a taxi for hire parked or even zipping past but neither materialized. He also considered riding the bus but was certain he would end up in Mazatlán because of his lack of language skills. The press of bodies on their way to appointments continued surrounding him, and noisy traffic rumbled a mere meter away from the concrete where his steps grew heavier with each rise and fall. The worn-out shoes seemed replaced by cement boots; his trousers hung onto his hips like laden sacks of grain. The sun was merciless, and Henry eventually succumbed, taking a seat on the curb beneath an Ahuehuete tree. Having been accustomed to Virginia, he was nearly defeated by the one-hundred-degree intensity. If not for the string of hope threading its way through his consciousness, he might have dozed off.

His elbows found a place to rest on his knees, and his forehead fell into his palms. Voices of passers-by trailed off into the background and car engines and scooter horns became a distant muffle. The urgency of finding Eduardo Elmar, his wife, and reuniting them with their son, was still in his mind. Pushing to the forefront was also the invitation from Congressman Samson he had accepted and turned his back on. It was so unlike him to make waves. He worried about sullying Josef's name with the congressman. If those stressors were not sufficient, the echoes of his bills called out. He had delayed the collectors which only compounded the interest he owed on small loans and monthly payments. The debt mounted with each day of Marie's illness, her medicine, the in-home care, her doctor visits. Each month was a debate of which bill would be paid and which had to wait. He did what he could, worked as many hours as possible, but never caught up. The cost of the funeral added to the liability balance. He would have gladly paid any amount to have his wife back, but the reality was that he didn't have her and there was a mountain of bills in her place.

He didn't have her. His beautiful Marie, who played beautiful music and had a beautiful voice, was gone. She could have chosen any man, yet, she had loved him. She sang to him, taught their daughter to play piano, taught their grandson to play her lovely melodies. She enriched his life and shared so many years of joy and struggle. He pursed his dry lips.

In the beginning, she was aware of what was happening, and fear gripped her. Henry would comfort her with a hug and a ready reassurance. He could always tell when a joke would be best or when to be quiet and just hold her. The last years, when she slipped away bit by bit, were difficult to endure. Near the end, when her spirit was gone and her body lingered, he was bolstered by the memories. He kept her alive with the deliberate recollections. His heart couldn't imagine life without her.

His head was heavy with discouragement. Marie was gone, and he could not change that fact. He was drowning with no signs of relief, which he compounded by abandoning Stuart Samson and incurring his own return flight arrangements. Without so much as a strategy, he struck out on this idealistic expedition to find and reunite a family. The reality had been harsh and the journey even more so for his sixty-seven-year-old non-athletic body. Now he faced the idea his strength was about to give out before he attained success. Negativity schemed to overtake his resolve. A wave of heat and oppressive car exhaust made his head swim. He closed his eyes and let his muscles relax; it would be so easy to let go.

The tiny voice of a child rescued him just before sleep tugged him under soothing waves.

"¿Naranja, senor?"

The orange was small and so was the boy's dirty hand. His face was a combination of dust and sweat and Henry saw in him the face of Mateo and Dimi all at once. The sight yanked him from the lull of despair into a determined posture.

"¿Senor?" He held it closer. *"Cinco pesos. Mmmm."*

"Si." Henry rose with a jerk and a stumble. His right hand slipped into the familiar pocket. He gave the boy some coins and accepted the orange. The smell that emanated when his fingers pierced the skin was enough to liven him before he even tasted the first wedge. The refreshing fruit piqued his tongue and the tip of his spirit. Juice dripped between his fingers. He felt the slightest tinge of renewal and his resolve labored back. It could have just been the sugar.

TWENTY-EIGHT

The building was smaller than Henry had expected, but he really hadn't known what to expect. The stucco was painted blue and had long since faded from the original hue. Cracks were evident, another culprit of torrid heat having dried up the basic composite of the masonry. The windows were plain glass without shutters or ornamental wooden framing. There was a single front door made of aluminum, and it was hanging precariously from the hinges. The structure looked like it might have been used for something else in the past, maybe a community center or a meeting hall. Smaller than a church, bigger than a house, the convalescent home had a worn metal sign in the front space with the words; Agape Centrar.

Henry carefully swung the worn-out door open and stepped inside. There was no one in the modest waiting room nor was the seat behind the reception desk filled. He looked for a bell, a buzzer, or some way to notify anyone that he was inside. He didn't see anything. He stepped toward one of two, perpendicular, tiled, hallways where the faintest of sounds could be detected. Not sure at first if it was a human voice or a television, Henry stepped toward the noise. A series of doors were positioned down the hallway that spanned nearly the length of the building. Trepidation clashed with the hope of finding Eduardo. Before he could teeter on that tightrope, a bouncy woman filled with swagger blasted out of one of the doors almost decking Henry in her wake.

"Ha," she laughed loudly. "Can I help ya?"

"I'm looking for Mr. Elmar. I was told he was transferred here from Regional Del Rio."

"Oh, ya, ya, he's right here. Come with." She wiggled and flounced her bulging bubble-gum pink uniform across the hall in front of Henry, pausing in front of room number nine.

"And you are?" She stopped to eye Henry up and down providing an ample deterrent before the door.

"I'm Henry Novak and I've been looking for him. I met his wife Rosa and son Mateo at the McAllen, Texas border station. I'm trying to reunite the family. It's been several days since I left the station and…" Henry blurted out the incoherent information, and the woman continued to scrutinize him as if having second thoughts. From a bed behind the woman came a mumbled string of Spanish words.

"Wait here," she directed.

Henry had no intention of moving.

The springy woman disappeared into the room, and Henry overheard a few low exchanges. She returned and stopped inches away from Henry's face. "Senor Elmar wans ta see ya, but don' ya dare upset him. I'm gonna' be right down the hall." She gave Henry an evil eye and left the door wide open while she bounced toward the lobby away from him.

It occurred to Henry that he didn't know what to say to the man in the bed. Where would he begin? A foolishness flooded through his veins as he realized his own inadequacy. Even though he had found Mateo's father, if indeed it was, what next? A complete wave of incompetence washed over him, and for a faint second, he hesitated about entering. Standing there motionless and ineffectual, he edged his gaze from side to side in search of guidance. He found it in the face of the lively woman who had been watching him from the end of the hall. She nodded in his direction, so he went in.

A slender man lay in a narrow bed with rumpled sheets and a thin pillow. His body made a small mound in the center of the mattress, and his right leg was in a cast, elevated by two more substantial pillows. Besides the cast, Henry noticed a splint on his right hand, fresh scars on his face and arms where stitches had recently been removed. Because of the ever-present heat, the top sheet was pushed to the man's waist, revealing gauze and tape around his chest and ribs soaked with sweat or something else. Dark hair was tousled and wedged against his head due to lapses of time resting on the clammy pillow.

Even though an air conditioning unit blared constantly from somewhere behind dusty vents, the room was muggy. Blinds were drawn to deter further heat from seeping in. A pitcher of ice water stood sweating on the old table between the two beds in the room. A second man snored loudly from the farther side. Henry stood half in the doorway with legs of lead.

Eduardo Elmar was looking up at the ceiling while Henry stood still. Both men were motionless for a time. The body in the farthest bed snored loudly, snorted, and startled himself into a bit more of a wakened state. He switched from his right side to his left and was now facing Mr. Elmar. He blinked and his eyes opened to fall to Henry.

Feeling the weight of the stare, Henry forced himself into the room. His quiet voice wavered with less confidence than an off-Broadway understudy.

"My name is Henry Novak. I was visiting at the border station in McAllen, Texas. I met your son Mateo and your wife Rosa."

Senor Elmar reacted to his family's names in the man's English.

"Rosa was released on May second. Did she come to see you? Did she find you?"

Senor Elmar raised his head the tiniest bit and tilted toward the man in the farther bed. In a rush of Spanish, the other man repeated Henry's words. Senor Elmar relaxed back onto the thin pillow.

"Si, Rosa estuvo aquí."

Henry recognized enough to understand she had found him. Trepidation fell off him instantly, and he approached the bed. The relief on his face was evident to the two men in beds. She had found him. Now *he* had found him, and perhaps her. It was a miracle. A grain of sugar in an ant hill.

"Do you know where she is?" Henry looked from one man to the other.

The other man translated and Senor Elmar simply nodded once. Encouraged, Henry explained what he hoped to accomplish; find her, reunite her with Mateo, reunite them all. He directed his words totally to the second man who was now fully awake, with his hairy legs hanging over the edge of his bed.

At some point, Henry realized his enthusiasm was not shared by either of the other men. He reined in his eagerness and asked about seeing her, talking with her. The other man did not translate but simply shook his head. Henry pushed. The translation came and was left hanging in the hot air. Henry searched each man's face.

"Sir?" he asked Senor Elmar. His incredulity mounted. Urgency returned to his fingers. He rubbed them on his pant legs before dismissing them to their pockets. "I want to help your family."

The man translated as Eduardo Elmar rose himself up with obvious discomfort. He winced and struggled with his injured body to erect himself and face Henry. In his own language he explained that his wife had found him yesterday. She was frantic, exhausted, and beyond consoling. She stayed for several hours, cried most of the time over their sons and their circumstances. She continues to fear the men who beat him and worries they are tracking the family. Her sister is still in Guatemala and now she fears for her safety as well. There is nowhere for them to go.

There is no money to pay for the hospital bills. There are too many people already here looking for jobs while they wait for their second hearing.

The words sunk in, and Henry reached out to the foot of the metal bed for stability. In the overwhelming situation of this family Henry sensed the misery. He again realized the futility of his good intentions. Without a plan, how could he have hoped to make a difference in this family's condition? What was he thinking? Happily, ever after? Even he doubted that now.

"Mr. Elmar, I still want to help. I don't know what I can do, but I must try to do something. I can't walk away. If you know where Rosa is, I would like to speak to her."

The translation was quick. It seemed that Senor Elmar was weighing the offer of help. He uttered a few words then the translation came.

"Rosa will be here sometime today. You can wait if you want to. I don't know how you'll help."

Henry accepted the words with the smallest amount of encouragement. He thanked both men, nodded his head several times, and backed out of the room. He stepped inside once more to repeat thank you and that he would be waiting out in the entrance area.

Henry settled into one of the two chairs in the reception area; choosing the one that looked less sticky. After he had rested for a few moments, the idea of thirst and hunger descended on him for the first time in many days. He was so thankful that he had succeeded in finding Mr. Elmar and realizing that Rosa would be along as well, his elation prevented fatigue from overcoming him completely. Instead, he rode the wave of excitement for as long as the adrenaline could pump through his veins. He fought the tears that threatened.

TWENTY-NINE

Rosa Elmar arrived at the Agape Center late in the afternoon. She was tired and hungry and frantic over her situation. The Mexican federal workers had been swamped. She needed them to plead her case to the American border patrol but the best she could achieve was an appointment for ten days out. There was the possibility that something might open sooner, but there was no way of knowing. She was welcomed to check back in a few days, but they made it clear, the more interruptions to check the schedule, the longer the wait would become.

She had managed to hide nine hundred pesos from the bandits and from the Americans but was afraid to use it for herself. What if she had to pay something for Mateo? Or Eduardo? She needed to keep the money safe and hidden. She had slid it into her sock, but now her foot was raw and hurting from walking on the coins. It would have to be okay for another day. Then, it would have to be okay the day after that.

Her hope was to get a Mexican official to call the border station and explain that her son was held by mistake. Even though she had expected to see Mateo when she was issued her hearing notification, he was not waiting there for her. She imagined he would be at the exit, smiling and happy to see her. By the time she realized no one had sent for him, she became hysterical and caused such a commotion, she was escorted out of the building. Agents explained that the policy was to send her son to the foster care agency while she waited for her second hearing. The confusion escalated until she was reduced to screaming Mateo's name while the guard physically ushered her to the Mexican side of the crossing.

The unpleasant memory of that episode was still vivid in her mind when she entered the nursing center and saw the old white man who sat slumped in a chair in the lobby. He snapped to attention when the door slammed. When he looked up and saw her, a smile crossed his face. She grew angry all over again at the sight of this American. Could he be coming for her? She was surprised she had enough energy to stoke rage.

"Rosa Elmar, I'm so glad to see you." He spoke, but all she understood was her own name. "I've been looking for you for days. I heard about you being returned and Mateo staying behind. I'm so sorry for this mistake. I want to help."

The man spoke hurriedly, and she didn't recognize anything but her son's name. She remembered vividly when he had come during her detention. The interpreter said he was some kind of important man dispatched from the American government. He talked to her. He told her he talked to Mateo. She did not know what any of it meant. Now he was here. *But why?* It couldn't be good.

He was moving closer to her. Rosa was uncomfortable. At least in the American enclosures she felt like she had a boundary. This…this was like being out on the road where the bandits beat Eduardo. She was alone, vulnerable. He was still coming with his hand reaching for her.

"Aléjate." Get away. She stepped back.

"I want to help you. Remember me? I'm Professor Henry Novak. We met at the detention center in McAllen, Texas. I was with several others. Mateo talked to me. I've been looking for you. We can go get Mateo." The man spoke but she didn't understand, nor did she trust him.

"No, me toques!" Rosa held her arms up, indicating she did not wish to make contact.

Henry paused, lowered his hands, and softened his voice. "I want to help reunite your family. Please, let me help you."

Rosa closed her eyes and twisted her hands. Her default was to run away, get herself safe. Without wasting time, reflex took over as she moved to the door and quickly opened it. She sensed the old man walking toward her, and it hastened her steps. She dashed outside and hurried around the side of the building before Henry could get to the door. She had no way of knowing that her actions usurped the last of his strength. She may have even pitied him if she had seen his sudden shallow breath, his shaking body, as he slumped backward into a chair.

* * *

The nursing home manager was thirty-nine years old, sixty inches high, and forty-five inches around. Her father was from Jamaica, but she had lived in Mexico her entire life. Camila Brown was proud to have been offered the managerial position and attributed her success to achieving an associate degree in nursing and having a bubbly personality. She commanded respect and tempered it with her sense of humor. A rare virtue in tough times, but an asset. Her vice was tobacco.

Even though she had cut down significantly, she continued to allow herself two short cigarette breaks each day during her ten-hour shift at Agape Centrar. It was her habit to step outside into the hot air and light her relaxer, walk leisurely around the building, enjoying her smoke. The walk and the smoke lasted about the same amount of time and it was a good combination. It cleared her head and congested her lungs.

About the time Camila was stamping out the flickering butt, a woman rushed around the building and bumped into her intimidating form. Both sputtered and stepped back. Camila looked at the flustered woman and recognized her from the day before.

"What's going on? Why are you running?" she asked Rosa Elmar in Spanish.

Out of breath, obviously rattled, the other woman stood gathering her wits. A quick jerk of Rosa's head over her left shoulder informed Camila that she was concerned about being followed. Camila waited for the other woman to calm herself but stood her ground, blocking retreat.

"A man is here from the American government," Rosa blurted.

"Yes, he came earlier and spoke with your husband. He wants to help you get your son back. He wants to reunite your family. I think he is a good man." Camila spoke the words, and her kind face peered into the eyes of the disheartened woman. She saw anger dwindle and the desperate body shrink inside its clothing. Camila worried Rosa might fall to the ground. Luckily, Rosa eventually nodded.

The two walked back to the entrance and stepped inside to find Henry Novak sitting on the edge of a chair, head above his knees. She indicated for the other woman to go to her husband, and she moved toward the man in the seat. She spoke gently to him, as if he were a patient. "Sir, are ya okay?"

The man did not look up. She could see the back of his neck but not the huge lump in his throat. She could see the thinning hair on his sunburned head but not the swell of tears under his eyelids. She was familiar with the posture, the tired pose of surrender. Some people snapped out of it, but she never could tell which ones it would be. A strong one might simply give up, and a weaker one might summon strength and persevere. This man was a stranger, and she didn't know his story nor his capability, but he was here, in her 'space,' and she was going to do what she could.

"Sir." She stretched her hand and lightly touched his shoulder. She could feel him heave a burdened sigh. "I'll be right back."

She bustled her vivacious frame around the corner of the reception counter and disappeared into the back of the nursing center. Minutes later, she returned with a tray of plastic cups and a steaming carafe. Henry had not shifted.

"Sir." Her voice was more persuasive. "Follow me."

Henry lifted his head out of his hands and looked toward the words he heard. He attended to the woman's command and rose to his feet. She led him to room number nine where Eduardo Elmar was lying in his bed and Rosa Elmar was standing next to his shoulder. Camila walked in and set the tray down, poured three cups of the steaming liquid, and offered one to each. Henry grasped his with both hands.

"You first." She nodded to Henry as she spoke in his language. He stared at her. "What do ya have ta say?" She encouraged him.

Camila observed the man holding the hot tea. He looked at her, to Rosa and Eduardo Elmar, and to the man snoring loudly in the far bed. He inspected his shoelaces for a short time, noticing the caked dirt. He raised the paper cup to his lips and blew the brew before sipping it.

"My name is Henry Novak, and I met your son, Mateo."

Camila looked at the husband and wife and repeated in their language.

THIRTY

There were a few candles, mildly scented of summer sand and eucalyptus, bunched on separate tables, flickering on the patio. Starlight bounced off the calm water in the pool giving the veranda a shimmering glow. The slightest hint of a melody wafted from one subtle speaker behind the well-stocked bar. An eight-foot fence surrounded the yard, embellished with hanging plants and growing shrubbery in full spring display.

Priscilla Harris-Hunt hired a landscaper to attend to the property. She detested servile work but appreciated a luscious yard. Occasionally, she took a liking to a good-looking pool boy. Tonight, there might be a boy in the pool, but his efforts would have nothing to do with cleaning it. The wicked vision made her smile.

This fling had lasted longer than previous distractions, and it occurred to her that she might be having too much fun, if it was possible. Did she dare carry on much longer? In the past her dalliances grew from boredom. Each of her previous involvements lasted long enough for her to feel she had conquered her quest and the intrigue dwindled afterward. The difference with this flirtation was that it had elements of romance. She felt she was getting to know this young man, and she actually enjoyed some things about him. He was intelligent and ambitious. He was definitely strong and handsome. And a fast study in the creative art of sensuality. She anticipated their liaisons, even planning little aspects that she hoped he'd like.

Lounging on her favorite creamy leather chaise, undressed in only her skimpy violet striped bikini, she examined her long slender salon waxed legs. Toenails matched fingernails detailed in a demure shade of salty pink. Hair was brushed back into a tempting style exposing her long neck where the hypnotic perfume that performed as well as any extracted pheromone was strategically dabbed, along with between her breasts and her inner thigh. She sipped a potent vodka and tonic while waiting, envisioning.

Jamison Corlander drove into the driveway at the now familiar address. He let himself inside the house as instructed and found his way through the spacious rooms to the back patio. He stopped outside the sliding glass doors, taking in the view, before saying hello.

"You're here. So glad tonight worked out for you." She purred, lifting, and swirling the ice in her drink. "Can I get you something?"

"Not yet. In a minute."

"Come, sit." She motioned to another lounge chair near her. "Tell me about your day." Her question amused her, and she stifled a tiny laugh.

"Not much to tell. Checked online for my grades. Thank you, by the way. Had a long practice. Hung out at my place for a while, and here I am." He smiled at her as he took a seat.

"You earned the grade," she said in an undetectable tone and shifted her head toward the pool. "Will you take summer classes?"

"I'm signed up for twelve credits, and I have football practice every day. It'll be busy. There won't even be much time to enjoy the two weeks between classes because of workouts." He was sitting sideways on the chair, facing her as she lay back. "Where is your husband this week?"

"He's off on a business trip to Dublin. I don't want to talk about him." She raised herself off the chair and moved to the bar. "Ready for a drink now?"

"Don't you ever want to go with him? I mean just to see the sights?"

"I've seen the sights. Been all over the world. Had the time of my life." It was hard to tell if she was being sarcastic or stating a fact. Without asking, she mixed him the same as what she was drinking. Holding the glass high, she jiggled it so the ice cubes would sound. Smiling her sweetest, she gestured for him to take the glass. He rose and came over.

He was taller than Priscilla, and she relished that variance. She liked peering up into his dark eyes and having him look over her body. She also enjoyed the musky smell of his skin against her, his sturdy arms around her; the undeniable masculine desire she sensed when he wanted her. It was a rare circumstance when she was dominated. She understood that she was intelligent and demanding and many men were not comfortable around her. Situations evolved when she had to assume control, when it was important for her to take charge. It was refreshing occasionally when someone else stepped in to lead the way--it made sex more fun.

He accepted the drink she mixed for him; sipped it once, took a beat, and sipped again. He reached his arm around her and rested the glass on the bar, freeing his hand to explore the tempting curve of her bare back. His fingers were strong yet tender as they played along her spine up to the blonde waves that ended near her delicately arched neck. He traced an invisible line along her shoulder until he lifted it from her arm and placed his entire hand on the small piece of material across her bum. She gasped when he pressed her closer until there was no space between them except for the fabric of their clothing.

Even though Priscilla had planned for this moment, imagined every move, the throes of the feelings overwhelmed her. This guy was such a potent temptation she stood weak in his arms. No matter how excited he became, how urgent his need for her, she wanted it more than he did, and it made her vulnerable. She had considered this fact several times in the last few weeks and refused to allow the possibility that it was true. However, right now, he was here, and she was about to let her ardent desire overtake her reservations.

She slipped her hands around his waist and pulled his shirt free. Her fingers snaked over him, pressing his skin lightly before she drew her nails across his back until his muscles flinched. The tie at the back of her bikini top loosened with his touch, and she stepped back to let it fall to the ground. While his eyes lusted over her, she unfastened his belt, unzipped his pants, and shook them down.

Before a heartbeat could pound, Jamison had shed his shirt and boxers. His embrace was fierce, and his mouth was voracious on hers. He continued to explore her flesh with warm strokes, and she melted under the contact. With an effortless gesture, he pulled the two chaises side by side and lay her on her back. He caressed her, excited her, ignited her, and shared carnal sex with her.

Priscilla loved that it took a long time. She loved that his chiseled body was virile, and his strong hands were slow. She loved that the sex was so amazing. Did she love *him*? Was this love or physical contact at its best? Whatever it was, it was good.

Clothing lay around the two lounge chairs. Bodies lay atop them. Time languidly passed.

"C'mon." He rose above her with his hand extended. She did not move. "C'mon."

She remained still. He bent over her small frame and picked her up as if she were weightless. When he inched toward the pool, she protested.

"No." He didn't stop. "Don't you dare." Her voice rose.

Jamison Corlander dropped the petite woman into the inviting water, saw her flail, and felt the splash spray against his bare legs. After she had bobbed to the top, he jumped in next to her with a huge smile on his face. She attempted to pummel his chest, but he caught both wrists and held them away. Still grinning, he moved closer to her. He released her arms, and she resumed the pounding while his fingers traveled around her moist body, drawing her curves firmly against him. Having prevented any injury her feeble blows might cause; he once again burned her lips with fiery kisses. She sizzled beneath the contact of his mouth. She felt his solid chest against her breasts, and it caused pulsing in her thighs. She raised her silky legs to wind around him. Passion was so hot that steam rose from atop the water.

The easy thrill of his powerful hands intensified the naughty designs she already entertained. He lifted her to the cool cemented edge of the pool. Wet drops slid across his naked physique while he climbed out, cradled her neck, and pressed her to the ground. His perfect body, with various cleat marks from adolescence and scars as recent as last month, was kneeling over her now, soaked and shining under the moonlight. He stroked her drenched hair, traced his finger over her delicate cheek, her slender neck, down her chest, not stopping at her navel. Each cell of her skin reacted to the contact of his fingers as if electrified.

The two lay at the side of the pool, damp and shivering from cool night air. Jamison softly rubbed his hand along her silken skin until its warmth transferred to her. Two bodies tangled along the ground in a sensuous embrace, and the rest of the world diminished in importance. A single kiss, the slightest smile, a twinkle in each eye. They had sex, he had his way, they made love.

* * *

"Tell me about the sights you've seen. You said you've been all over the world. Like where?" Jamison hadn't been anywhere outside of the U.S. It was fascinating to him to think that she had.

"Everywhere." Priscilla's answer was flat.

"Give me some names."

Priscilla poured herself another drink. Her hair was still slicked back from pool water and her curvaceous body was warming beneath a velvet robe. He hadn't noticed that her makeup had washed off in the pool, or that her mascara was smeared; she still managed to look stunning in his eyes. It didn't even register that the seductive perfume that twisted him inside out had rinsed away with the ripples in the water. He was living in the moment, enchanted.

"I've been to Ontario, Canada several times. Vancouver, which is breathtakingly beautiful. Nova Scotia. Mexico a few times on vacation; Cancun, Puerto Vallarta, Cabo San Lucas. Belize. Barbados. Jamaica. Bahamas. Puerto Rico. Curacao. Aruba. Those were mostly vacationing during cold Virginia winters—breaks between semesters.

"I've been to Egypt and South Africa. I've been to Sydney. Been to Italy, France, Germany, Spain, England, Ireland. Yea, a lot of places." She swirled the ice in her glass and seductively reclined on the creamy leather lounge chair. "That's most of it I guess."

"What was your favorite?"

"Oh, come on. They're so different. It's hard to compare."

"Okay, tell me something amazing about some of them. What did you do there, what did you like? Did anything make you smile?" His unabated interest shone through the timbre of his voice. Imagining the adventures intrigued him.

"Which do you think would be an interesting place?" She was teasing him now.

"Africa."

She repositioned herself back against the chaise, drew one slender leg up till her knee peeked through the robe, and sipped her drink. Her head tilted back before she answered.

"When our ship docked in Alexandria, there were soldiers with rifles standing at the dock. That was a bit off-putting when you step off a ship and there are armed men. We passed by them to go into the city. There were beggars near the harbor. Men pushed their crying children to the front, for pity, and money. There were some wonderful sights. We went to Cairo. Traveled parallel to the Nile until we reached Giza and the pyramids. Saw the Sphynx. In the museums were mummies, artifacts, ancient tools, pottery, and jewelry."

"That's fantastic."

"It was hot there. No air conditioning in the museums. Lots of sand blowing around. Desert, you know. And the food was not what I was used to."

"Were you impressed? You had to be overwhelmed by the historical aspect."

"Of course."

"What about Italy?"

"What about it?"

"Where did you go, what did you see?

"Rome, and all of the sights that come to mind; the Vatican, the Coliseum, Trevi Fountain, Spanish Steps. We went to St. Mark's Square in Venice, went to Florence. And by the way, Michelangelo's David has nothing on you, Sugar." There was no feature in her voice; her words were vapid. She may as well have been listing groceries. She wasn't even looking in his direction.

Jamison was hardly aware of her disinterest. He was enthralled by the idea of travel and the sounds of the places she had visited. So engrossed was he in the ideas of those cities, historical places, monuments, and art, that he couldn't think of what to ask. He could only say, "Tell me more."

"Jamison, honey, after a while, the airplane takes off, the airplane lands, and you're just in a different place. There are touristy things to see everywhere. You try the food, the wine, you walk around. Believe me, it gets tedious." She sipped from the glass in her hand, unaware of herself jingling the ice.

"And France," he asked as if he hadn't heard her disparaging words. "Did you go to Paris? Did you go to the Louvre? Did you see the Mona Lisa? What about the Champs-Élysées? Eiffel Tower?"

"Yes."

"And…"

"Everyone smokes in Paris. They allow dogs in restaurants but leave babies in carriages outside on the pavement. The Mona Lisa is the size of a postage stamp. The Eiffel Tower had to be repaired, and they reinforced it so it would deliberately lean otherwise there would be no reason for anyone to ever go to Pisa."

"The Eiffel Tower or the leaning tower?"

"Yes, of course, the leaning tower. The Eiffel Tower was erected so Mr. Eiffel could build the tallest building at the time and draw World Fair goers to France. Kind of a macho endeavor, so to speak." The restlessness in her mood was beginning to show.

The information combined with the wondrousness of the scope of these travels amounted to somewhat of a dream for Jamison. He couldn't imagine himself seeing these historic places, and yet, he was with someone who had literally been there. The dull tone of her voice was beginning to reach him. He sat next to her.

"It sounds wonderful. How exciting for you. I would love to take a trip like that--with you." The sincerity only exaggerated the age difference. He wasn't aware that he sounded like, well, like a schoolboy, and she the world-travelled professor. Imaginings of the exotic locations were still circling through his mind when Priscilla rose, and wobbled. He steadied her with an outstretched arm. Rising beside her, he guided her to her bedroom, where she then insisted, he go on while she excused herself to the en-suite.

He did as she directed. Let himself out, locked the front door at the electronic keypad, and drove off toward campus. Dreams of travel, culture, adventures, accompanied him over the route to his place with a promise that he would see it all someday. Next time he would think of specific questions to ask. It was great when they actually talked.

THIRTY-ONE

The initial impression that Henry Novak got from Sergeant Basil Cayne when they met a week before, was that he was a straightforward, plain-speaking guy. If it was accurate, Sean Hennesy was all that, to Mars and back. Hennesy was a man of few words, and when he did speak, the comments were short, not sweet, and direct. For the last eighty minutes, Henry had listened to the man arrow through conversations with accelerated aplomb. Directing questions and piecing puzzles seemed to be aspects of his job, although Henry wasn't sure exactly what his title was or what his credentials were. The only certainty was that Sergeant Cayne had told him to have a seat, and a few minutes later Hennesy walked in.

Henry had nothing to hide. He was of a mind that everyone already heard what he had tried to do. It was his assumption that Hennesy had the answers to the questions before he asked them. It occurred to him this was a CYA situation, and he was expected to relieve ICE, the Center for Border Protection, and Border Patrol, from responsibility surrounding his actions. He was more than willing to cooperate. Every inquiry was met with the truth to the best of Henry's recollection. He admitted some of his time in south Texas and Mexico was foggy. Depression can rob you in many ways.

Ever since Sean Hennesy entered the room, he shot off questions while standing or pacing. Henry wasn't certain if the stone man was tired or satisfied with the answers, but after an hour and some, Hennesy sat on one of the uncomfortable molded plastic chairs. Henry's eyes remained on the other man in anticipation of more queries. Hennesy looked at his phone. Voices rose just outside the door before it opened. Rosa Elmar stepped in along with Sergeant Basil Cayne and Liza Booker who had interpreted for the congressional team.

Henry's eyebrows knotted. Watching each of the persons as they entered the room, he could not calculate what might be presenting itself there. He waited silently. The tension in the room was elevated by heat and perspiration; a common mixture this time of year. The overhead light blared so brightly that it tired Henry's eyes and made his hair hurt. He felt like a bag of wet sand while he sat in the uncomfortable chair. Sergeant Cayne spoke in a manner that resembled his stature; curt and condensed.

"Professor Novak, I grasp that you were trying to find this woman and reunite her with her son because you thought a mistake had been made." While he spoke, Liza softly translated to Rosa in a corner of the room. "It distresses me that you set out on your own before clarifying the situation. Still, what's done is done." He was standing midway across the room looking directly at Henry. With a bit more volume in his voice he asked, "Do you know how lucky you are that nothing happened to you?"

It was not the first time it occurred to Henry that he may have been in danger. The wandering days of minimal food, water, and rest moved through his mind. In retrospect, he had done a stupid thing by striking out alone on a half-baked idea of pursuit. The concept that he had found Eduardo and Rosa astounded even *him* now. Hindsight of the last days allowed for him to appreciate the enormity of the undertaking.

"Yes sir, I believe I do."

"Your actions have put not only you, but me and this agency in a negative light since it was the congressman who had arranged for your visit. You are aware that your departure flight left days ago." It was not a question, so Henry did not respond. Sergeant Cayne continued to stand in an erect fashion; veins in his thick neck were pulsing. His words were delivered with sufficient gravity. Henry was getting the message.

"A deluge of immigrants has led to a tremendous backlog at our station. Refugees are scaling the wall and tunneling under it daily. We have families waiting for proper processing and hundreds without adequate applications. Let us be clear. Mistakes are made because of sheer volume. Your disappearance has leveled a spotlight on what will be interpreted as an unforgiveable incident." His words were chosen with care.

"I am not proud that this oversight was made, and I will correct it, you have my word. But the federal government must know that I *am* proud of the work done here and the degree of excellence that all of our team members display."

Liza continued to translate the words to Rosa who listened with interest.

Henry sat stiffly, like an errant child being scolded. Part of him felt that he deserved it, another part of him bristled. He kept his eyes on Sergeant Cayne, uncertain if he should look away or not.

"Your entire reason to leave your group was to locate this woman. Is that correct?"

Henry had answered this question in a dozen of its variations, but he dared not state that. "Yes."

"Your sole motivation was that you wanted to reunite them. Correct?" Sergeant Cayne's agitation was distinct.

"Yes, sir. I met each of them during my stay here. It was incredible that it even happened. Just before leaving to return to D.C., I visited the tents, and Mrs. Elmar was gone, but Mateo was still here. I was trying to find her because it was my belief, they were supposed to go to a foster place together to wait."

"You now recognize that you were wrong in your assumption." Sergeant Cayne had a way of making a question sound like a statement that didn't invite an answer. Instead of shooting off another round of questions, the sergeant bent his head as if to make sure his boots were adequately shiny. Dust covered them. He peered into Henry's face with penetrating eyes, rubbed his bald head and stomped around in a circle where he stood, then looked across the small room at Hennesy. The bomb exploded. "How in *hell* did you *find one woman* in the *throngs* of *all* the *people* congregated *across the border*?" Sergeant Cayne's question boomed to a decibel that jarred Henry.

Weary from the long interrogation and the days leading up to it, he squirmed uncomfortably in the molded plastic chair. "It was a miracle or something very close."

There was now a total of five people in the room who had been woven together through a web of coincidence. Their brief interaction brought them to this room from their long personal journeys and drastically different origins. Henry took a breath. He sensed the heat of their eyes on him. Gathering his nerve, considering his words, he spoke in a feeble tone. "May *I* ask a question?"

The Sergeant huffed, nodded, and glanced toward Hennesy, who appeared to be monitoring phone messages.

"Does the family have a sponsor? Is there any chance they will be accepted into the U.S.?" Henry asked.

"Mrs. Elmar and Mateo arrived without sponsorship or application papers. They do have adequate I.D., but they are attempting to show they are in danger if returned to their home. There was a homicide in the family that is under investigation, which takes time. Mrs. Elmar had her initial appearance before the judge. Now they wait for our investigation. The chances are 50/50 that they'll be allowed to come in, but there's a long line ahead of them."

"I would like to sponsor the family if they are willing. Can I do that?"

"Excuse me?" Sergeant Cayne took a small step forward. Again, he looked to Hennesy, who did not meet his eyes.

"How do I begin the process? Can you direct me?"

Someone cleared his throat, someone sucked air. A faint whimper escaped from a timid voice while Henry trained his eyes on the trembling hands in his lap. Rhythmically, a second hand swept around a dial as if blurting out a countdown in the tight room. Henry realized the need for a breath but could not force his lungs to work. With trepidation, he angled his head toward Rosa and tried to read her face. Next, he searched Sergeant Cayne's posture for some sort of clue. He met the glaring stare of Sean Hennesy as the man stood up.

"Are you serious?" Hennesy posed a looming figure in his full height and his voice carried a grave tone.

"Yes, sir."

Sean Hennesy looked like a wall; stone hard, and unyielding. There was no interpreting what was going on inside his regimented mind, what thoughts he harbored, and what, if any, emotion he might experience. If looks could kill, Henry would be tasered and lasered. He was certain he was about to die just from the man's stare.

The second hand continued its trek around the clock's face. The nerves of each individual were taut with anticipation and some dread. What would he say? Would he refuse? Could he refuse? Could it be done? Why would he agree? *What was I thinking*? That was Henry. Everyone waited until they expected to burst and, finally, Hennesy spoke.

"More goddam paperwork."

[2019]

THIRTY-TWO

The summer semester had been long and tougher than Jamison Corlander expected. He took the twelve credit hours on top of his double practices and found himself exhausted by the end of each day. The classwork was a gear shift from push-ups, squats, and sprints. One exercised his brain to fatigue while the other did the same to his muscles. It was a seesaw of balance, up or down or just in mid-air. He probably concentrated on football more than book work.

The coach promised a grueling fall season, and he wasn't kidding. The roster was a tough series of matchups but 'when you play the best you bring your best.' Jamison just wanted to show his talent, show what he could do, that he had what it took to make it to the pros. In his final college season, his efforts were going to pay off. Nothing was going to distract him. This was the home stretch.

A bit more than half-way through the season, game seven, he wrenched his ankle running for the end zone. The manager got on it right away; iced it, taped it. Jamison wanted to get back in the game, but the coach said no. Said there were five more games. Said he was needed for those, and he had to sit out for the last twelve minutes of this one. You must listen to the coach, even if you're pissed.

X-rays in the locker room showed a slight fracture. That meant out for maybe two or three weeks. No practice, no games. He studied. It was during this convalescence that he figured out who had gone to the dean and he realized he hadn't seen Sondra Mercer on campus in months.

By the time the football season ended, he had rehabbed and gotten in the last three games. He could tell he was not a hundred percent but prayed the scouts couldn't see it. His coach said there were a couple of calls about him, some interest. He waited and hoped. Tampa Bay wanted to look at him. In the end, it was the only attention he got. His excitement escalated. His adrenaline rose each time he pictured himself meeting the Buccaneer staff in Florida at the end of the month. Four weeks was a long time and he worked hard at holding his excitement and anxiety in check.

For now, he was glad to be done. Done with practices, done with exams and research papers, done with cold Virginia weather. It was time to relax, he told himself, he deserved it.

The temperature in Santorini in January was sixty degrees. Not warm enough for sunbathing but perfect for sight-seeing. He was dressed in tan linen slacks and a coral color Henley. Standing along the amazing archeological excavation at Akrotiri, he felt the significance of this ancient cultural site. Ropes prevented enthusiasts from interfering with the actual dig, yet there, in plain view, were unearthed tools, vessels, benches, even parts of buildings from the 17th century B.C. His excitement increased with each step, each new museum, each blue-domed church, and white-washed house.

The Red Beach at the bottom of the spectacular red cliff wall was bordered in its brilliance by the sapphire sky and the turquoise water like an elegant frame enhances a beautiful portrait. These sights would always persist in his memory. How could anyone forget the splendor? He eagerly walked the entire day, taking in the magnificence and wonder. He talked long into another excited night about every spectacle and the depth of his awe. It was an elaborate dream realized.

"I do believe you're having fun."

"I believe I am." She clinked the ice in her vodka and tonic.

"It must have been those ethics sessions during your furlough. Naughty professor. Have you reformed?

"Of course, I have. Can't you tell?

"All that time alone, away from your students. Do you suppose it made you want a change in scenery?"

"It might have been that. It might have been that I needed to get some sun. It might have been that I just needed to show you some sights. You needed a little cultural exposure before you're off to be a football star." "So, you wanted to 'expose' me? Is that what I'm hearing?"

"Sugar, you know how I feel about exposing you."

"Well, I think you're having fun, and I believe you're seeing things differently; more appreciatively."

"That's a big word."

"Well, if you're impressed by something big, you're gonna love this…"

Jamison took slow steps toward Priscilla and caught the fire in her eyes through a warmth in his own. He eased himself next to her silky skin that had been alluringly kissed by a Mediterranean breeze and inhaled the heady smell of her. His unrelenting gaze held her eyes while he tempered the strength in his hand to stroke her cheek. The beat of his heart sped up as it always did when they lay this close. Before he would please her, he wanted to hold her. Before she would moan with satisfaction, he wanted to savor their simple affection.

Greece fostered an idyllic end to an unrealistic match-up. The beauty and history provided a backdrop for a romance that would abruptly self-destruct within the next few days. The thrill of the fantasy would linger in his heart with each extraordinary memory of the passionate sensations from their forbidden involvement.

"Thank you," he whispered into her delicious neck, pulling her intimately close, breathing her in one more time. Before she could ask what for, he made good on his promise of something big.

[2021]

"Yo pon el tenedor sobre la mesa."

"Yo pon el tenedor sobre la mesa," Henry repeated before Dimi took his turn. Henry smiled at his grandson, but the boy looked to his teacher.

"Bueno." Mateo gently smiled at both. He raised the fork and placed it on the table to validate their words. Next, he picked up a spoon and asked, *"¿Que es esse?"*

"Cuchara!" Dimi shouted before his grandfather could summon the translation for spoon.

"Muy bueno." The two boys bumped fists then elbows.

"¿Disculpe?" Henry asked to be excused. It was his night as cook and the pot of potatoes was boiling over. The boys continued the lesson as he rose and turned to the stove, picked up a large spoon, and a thick towel.

The gray living room that was now a living room again, and an office, and a closet, housed blue plastic crates, books, papers, and research manuals. A stiff cardboard box held some boys' corduroy pants, jeans, shirts, socks, and Spiderman underwear. Another cardboard box held men's socks, boxers, work pants, work shirts, and a belt. A green rubber tote stacked on top of the others held blouses, slacks, under things, a pair of walking shoes, and a pair of work shoes. The four moved around the small apartment navigating its obstacle course. Each had their own household tasks, everyone's paychecks were needed to make ends meet, each made room for the others, and no one complained.

Dimi visibly lit up when he visited Mateo enjoying all the different things there were to do. They enthusiastically exchanged language lessons, played Roblox on Dimi's old computer, watched videos in English, and had a lively catch with a favorite red rubber ball. He could hardly wait for the time when he would teach what he learned at the piano. It was almost like having a brother, but not exactly. Dimi learned to stay quiet when the shadow came over Mateo's face. He eased back when the older boy cried. He had heard something about nightmares. It was infrequent, and therefore special, when they shared a hug.

The legal process had taken a long time and cost his grandfather a lot of money. The last round of papers, payments, and court dates had taken place a few months before, but not without the endless snafus and delays that had come to be expected in the procedure. His grandfather's commitment had remained staunch throughout the course. Dimi had overheard pieces of grown-up conversations regarding terrible things that happened to his new family. In his young mind, he attempted to make sense of how they had suffered and known loss. He realized that, in a way, *he* was filling a hole, even if he didn't recognize how or why. It was okay to not comprehend grown-ups and their adult lives. His father had told him that he would understand in due time, and he trusted his father. He came to believe that a hollow cavity inside his grandfather was also healing. There was noisy life in the old apartment, newly crowded with three more people, with busy work schedules, and a hectic school calendar. Healing was especially evident on the elder man's wrinkly face when music played, when spontaneous laughter rang out, and on the rare occasion that Rosa quietly hummed while folding clothes.

POSTFACE

In 1985, Jenny Lisette Flores, an unaccompanied fifteen-year-old girl fleeing war in El Salvador, was apprehended by the Immigration and Naturalization Service (INS) after illegally attempting to cross the Mexico-U.S. border. A Hollywood actor called his lawyer, Carlos Holguín, to get help for his maid's daughter from El Salvador.

In 1997, Democratic President Bill Clinton signed the Flores Settlement Law that required unaccompanied minors who arrived in the U.S. to be released to their parents, a legal guardian, or an adult relative. If no family members were available, the relevant government agency could appoint an appropriate adult to look after the child. The Flores Settlement also importantly set a standard for their care and limited how long the government could hold migrant children.

In 2005, Republican President George W. Bush introduced Operation Streamline which referred for prosecution immigrants illegally crossing the border but made an exception for parents with children. In 2008, President Bush signed an anti-trafficking statute that required unaccompanied minors to be transferred out of immigration centers within seventy-two hours. Neither of the Clinton nor Bush administrations recommended separating families.

After a surge of families from Central America started arriving at the U.S. south-western border in 2014, Democratic President Barrack Obama opened family detention centers. That prompted criticism and lawsuits arguing the move breached the Flores Settlement by not releasing children swiftly.

In November 2014, President Barrack Obama implemented a "Common-Sense Immigration Policy" which allowed about forty-five percent of illegal immigrants to legally stay and work in the U.S. The proposal provided undocumented immigrants already living in the U.S. a legal way to earn citizenship which was; pass national security and criminal background checks, pay taxes and a penalty, and learn English before earning citizenship.

In December 2014, a U.S. District federal judge ruled President Obama's executive action was unconstitutional. Following injunctions and appeals, the Secretary for Homeland Security, John F. Kelly, announced on June 15, 2017 that the order establishing the "Deferred Action for Parental Accountability" program was rescinded. President Obama deported more than two million immigrants during two terms in office.

In 2016, the Ninth Circuit Court of Appeals ruled the Flores Settlement "unambiguously" applies to both minors who are accompanied and unaccompanied by their parents. It also overturned a Federal District Court's decision that the government must also release the parents.

Before 2017, records were not required by the court. Since 2017, upwards of three thousand children have been reportedly separated from their families; the number could have hit thousands more than reported. While the George W. Bush and Barrack Obama administrations did break up families, it was reportedly rare according to officials and immigration experts. From March 2017 to March 2018, the Department of Homeland Security reported a two-hundred-three percent increase in illegal border crossings.

In April 2018, during Republican Donald J. Trump's administration, the Attorney General, Jeff Sessions, announced its "Zero-Tolerance Policy" which prohibited both attempting and entering the country illegally; described as "new" and in response to an increase in unauthorized border crossings that spring. The policy called for criminal prosecution of everyone who enters the country illegally. As a result, more than three thousand children were forcibly separated from adult family members who were detained under the new policy, which President Trump officials have characterized as a deterrent.

On June 26, 2018, a federal judge in San Diego, responding to an American Civil Liberties Union (A.C.L.U.) lawsuit, directed the federal government to halt the separation at the border and to reunite children with their parents. President Donald Trump rescinded the policy the same month.

The setting of this book is 2018, at which time Carlos Holguín continued the work he began in 1985, fighting for rights of immigrant minors.

AUTHOR'S NOTE

While watching cable news roughly two years ago a scene unfolded that grabbed my attention. The commentary has long since left my memory but the visual will be forever etched on my cortex. A father and mother were ushered into a tight area where an agent was waiting with their small child. A separation had taken place and a joyous reunion was expected. The mother was thrilled to see her little one and rushed forward. Against probability, the child rejected his parents. The mother excitedly bent with open arms only to be rebuffed repeatedly, resulting in her dissolution into mournful shrieks. The father, equally unnerved, hung back. Over and over the mother reached for her frightened child and as many times, the child declined contact. Unnatural sounds of anguish rose from the mother after each snub, rendering the scene equally difficult to hear and witness. That was the compelling incident around which Separated was shaped. Even though the Elmar family were prominent characters, the two that I called Verdi and Francisco were the catalysts for the novel. My hope is that I was able to depict the distress that was so apparent to me when I viewed the news clip and represent the torment through my words on the page.

Psychologists have long understood that reattachment after unexpected displacement is real and the effects can be devastating. Although trauma is universal, everyone's experience of it is unique. It is impossible to predict who will possess the resiliency to heal, and who will be harmfully changed.

Many months of discriminating research went into the detail of fashioning a story about the immigration crisis. A trip to McAllen, Texas was planned before the pandemic prevented travel and safety of such an excursion. Be certain that facts were dutifully verified in all instances where possible and only reputable sources were used to shape the fictious events.

ACKNOWLEDGEMENTS

Many people are involved behind the scenes whenever a book makes it to print. My thanks go out to Tom Montgomery and Randy Cardenas who are treasured beta-readers and provided significant feedback during the early stages. Pat Theiler, a long-time friend, offered valuable input about the workings of the Office of Refugee Resettlement and varied government departments which pointed me in a better direction. Recognition credit to Bear who posed for the cover. I appreciate my friends who write and encourage me with tales of trial and success. My gal-pals are a source of endless support for which I am beyond grateful. Family has been a blessing with abundant backing and reassurance. Last, but in no way least, my husband of fifty years is my first-round editor, suggestion provider, patient listener, idea wall to be bounced off, and partner in all stages of writing, who I couldn't begin to repay.